Land of Soul

Where Shadows Teach and Light Transforms

Toya Kraft

Kraft Publishing Enterprises LLC

Published by Kraft Publishing Enterprises LLC

ISBN: 979-8-9955386-0-8

Cover design by Toya Kraft

Interior design by Toya Kraft

Printed in the United States of America

For LaVance and LaTrice Colley and the Ones learning to work with their shadows and trust their own light again

Reader's Note: How to Use This Glossary

This glossary is not meant to define your experience for you. It is here to support it.

The language of ***Land of Soul*** blends metaphor, emotion, and inner landscapes. Some terms describe places within the story; others describe inner states you may recognize in yourself. None of them are meant to be interpreted as diagnoses, judgments, or fixed truths.

Use this glossary in whatever way feels right:

As a **companion** when a word or symbol stirs something in you As **grounding** when a chapter feels emotionally dense

As **reflection** when you want to understand how the story mirrors your own inner world

As **permission** to explore at your own pace There is no "correct" meaning here.

Each definition is an **invitation** — a doorway into your own understanding. Let the words meet you where you are.

Table of Contents

Prologue – THE LAND OF SOUL (The Fracture)

The journey did not begin with a step. It began with a stirring.

Long before the Dark Land cast its shadow, before the River of Process whispered its first warning, something quiet awakened within the souls who would one day cross its threshold. It was not fear, nor certainty, but a subtle pull — the kind that rises when life can no longer remain what it has been.

The Land of Soul had always been a place of harmony, a realm where light and shadow lived in delicate balance. Yet every soul, no matter how rooted, carried a moment when the familiar no longer fit. A moment when the heart felt both the ache of what was and the call of what could be.

For some, the stirring came as a restlessness. For others, as a heaviness.

For a few, as a quiet knowing that change was already unfolding.

No one recognized it at first. Not the healers, nor the musicians, nor the dreamers who charted constellations in the night sky. But the River of Process felt it. Its waters shifted, carrying a new current beneath the surface

— a current that would soon touch every life in the land.

This is where the journey truly begins:

not in the Dark Land, not in the trials that await, but in the moment a soul realizes it can no longer remain unchanged.

The path ahead will ask much — courage, honesty, and surrender. It will reveal shadows long avoided and light long forgotten.

It will test the stories each traveler has carried and the truths they have yet to claim. But the journey is not punishment. It is invitation.

Chapter 1: THE CALL OF THE RIVER

The first light of dawn touched the land, casting golden rays over the rolling hills of the Land of Soul. The sky stretched wide in soft hues of pink and lavender as the sun, rising slowly and steadily, began to warm the earth with quiet intention. Morning did not rush here; it unfolded.

The River of Process wound gently through the landscape, a flowing current that both calmed and stirred. Its waters shimmered like molten glass beneath the growing light, reflecting not only the sky above but the unseen currents beneath the surface. It never stood still. Even in its stillness, it moved.

In this place of light and cultivated peace, Solana walked among the meadows. Her steps were unhurried, deliberate, as she listened to the pulse of the earth beneath her feet. The air carried the scent of blooming jasmine, and distant birdsong drifted like a hymn across the fields. Wherever she passed, the atmosphere seemed to soften. Her presence was not loud or commanding, yet it shifted things — like sunlight slipping through a window.

Serenity was not merely something she offered it was something she embodied.

She greeted the creatures of the land with a warm and inviting smile, reminding all who encountered her that peace was not simply a gift bestowed upon the fortunate. It was a choice made daily, often quietly, and sometimes with great courage.

Beneath a flowering tree sat a young soul, their gaze distant, uncertain. Their eyes shimmered with unspoken doubts, a heart weighed down by questions too heavy for their years. Solana knelt beside them. With a gentle hand resting upon their shoulder, she spoke softly, her voice like a breeze that stirs but does not disturb.

"Peace is not the absence of challenges," she said. "It is the embrace of them, knowing they are part of your journey. The light will always find its way — no matter how dark the night."

The youth's breath steadied. Something within them shifted — not completely healed, not entirely resolved — but steadied. And sometimes that is where transformation begins.

***

Solana by the River

Dawn came like a slow unbuttoning, the sky easing from indigo to the soft pink of a bruise healing. Solana walked the riverbank with bare feet, letting the cool mud press between her toes. The River of Process moved in its steady, secret way — not loud, not showy, but carrying everything it touched. She cupped her hands and let the water run through them, watching the light break into a thousand small, obedient stars.

There was a habit she kept, a small liturgy no one else knew. She would stand until the sun had warmed her shoulders, then she would whisper the names of those she could not save. It was not a prayer for forgiveness; it was a naming, a way to keep their faces from dissolving into the fog of duty. Today the list came back to her like a tide: a child with a fever, a mother who refused to rest, a man who laughed too loud to be believed. Each name was a stone she had carried and set down, only to pick up again.

She remembered the child most clearly. He had been small enough to fit in her lap, his breath a fragile bell. The fever had come like a thief, quick and merciless. She had done everything she knew — poultices, songs, the slow turning of the body to ease the heat — but the fever kept climbing like a stubborn vine. The night he died, she had sat with his mother until the stars blurred. The mother's hands were empty of the child's weight, and Solana had felt a hollowness open in her chest that no remedy could touch.

Afterward she had promised herself two things: never to let a name fade, and never to pretend that healing was a tidy thing. She had learned that healing could be a small, stubborn tending — a hand on the shoulder, a bowl of warm broth, a silence that held grief without trying to fix it. That promise had become a ritual: each dawn she named the lost, and each dusk she lit a small lamp for the living.

A breeze moved through the reeds and carried with it the scent of jasmine from the meadow. The memory softened but did not leave. Her hands trembled as she set the water down and pressed her palm to the river's surface. "You carry them," she said aloud, not to the river but to the space between her ribs where the names lived. "Carry them with me."

The river answered in its own way — a ripple, a small brighting where the sun touched the water. It was not consolation; it was recognition. Solana let herself feel the ache without trying to smooth it. She had learned that the ache was not a defect but a doorway. It taught her what to hold and what to let go.

A child's laugh drifted from the village, bright and careless, and for a moment the world tilted toward ordinary things: bread baking, a dog's bark, the clumsy joy of someone learning to dance. She smiled, small and private, and the smile felt like a stitch.

Solana gathered a handful of river stones and tucked them into the pocket of her robe. Each stone was a name, a memory, a promise. She would carry them until the day she could set them down without the weight of guilt. For now, they were ballast — reminders that to heal was to keep remembering, to keep tending, to keep being present for the small, stubborn work of mending.

The land was waking, and with it, the quiet work of the day. She would meet people, mend what she could, and when night came she would light her lamp and whisper the names again. The ritual was simple and endless, and in its repetition she found a kind of grace.

Solana paused to admire the land as it awakened. The fields seemed to pulse with life. Dew clung to the grass like scattered stars reluctant to leave. Every corner of Soul appeared touched by radiance.

She folded the last lamp into a scrap of cloth and tucked it into her satchel, then walked the lane toward the miller's stoop. The ledger lay open where the miller had left it—names and measures penciled in a cramped, tired hand. Solana set the lamp on the page and smoothed the paper with her thumb as if calming a restless child. A neighbor came out carrying a jar of broth, shoulders tight from a night of hauling water. They did not speak of grief; they traded a single, practical thing — broth for a promise to check the roof before the next storm.

The exchange was quiet and adult: no speeches, no grand consolations, only the small economy of people who keep one another alive. The miller's fingers closed around the lamp, then the ledger, then the jar. He did not look up to meet Solana's eyes; instead, he tied the ledger closed with a strip of twine and set it under his arm as if the act of securing the list could steady the world.

Solana rose and walked on, the lamp warm against her ribs like a small, honest truth. She passed the blacksmith's shop where a man sat on the step, hands empty of tools. He watched the river as if it might tell him what to do next. She did not offer a sermon. She set the lamp on the step beside him and, with a motion practiced from years of tending, smoothed the calluses on his palm with the heel of her hand. The man's jaw loosened. He picked up his hammer and tapped it once against the anvil — a sound that was not triumph but a promise to return to work.

The river kept its slow, secret song. Solana walked back toward the clearing, the lamp's warmth a small ballast. The ritual of naming had not changed the world. It had only made a place for the work that would follow:, lists to be checked, roofs to be mended, meals to be shared. That was the kind of tending that held a village together.

She knew her purpose here was greater than healing wounds. It was to remind others that peace was not a destination one finally arrived at. It was a way of being.

Not far from the meadow's edge, Aurelian stood by the River of Process, watching the water ripple and swirl. His presence was firm, grounded — strength without aggression. A warrior in his own right, he understood the delicate balance between light and dark, peace and turmoil. His role was not to destroy the shadows. It was to ensure that neither shadow nor light overwhelmed the other.

He studied the river carefully, sensing patterns invisible to most. When Solana approached, he turned to her with a solemn expression.

"The river," he said, his voice deep and thoughtful, "flows steady

today. But I can feel a shift in the currents. Something stirs in the distance

— like the warning of a storm yet to come."

Solana's gaze followed the movement of the water. Though her face

remained calm, she too felt a subtle tension in the air, like a held breath.

"We are guardians of this realm, Aurelian," she replied evenly. "But even we cannot prevent the storms of life. They are inevitable. And they bring growth. The river will carry us through whatever is to come."

From the edge of the nearby forest, Seraphiel emerged. The healer and guide moved with quiet grace, their presence both gentle and profound. Wisdom rested in their eyes — deep, reflective, timeless. Like the river itself, Seraphiel carried a quiet strength capable of healing wounds both seen and unseen.

"I sense it too," Seraphiel said, their voice soft as wind weaving through leaves. "But remember — the greatest healing often comes through struggle. We will guide the souls of this land not only through peace, but through the storm as well."

Together, the three stood by the river. They watched as its waters moved with purpose — sometimes serene, sometimes turbulent. They had seen this before: how swiftly life could shift; how the flow could surge with power, testing all who stood in its path; how, at other times, it would slow, inviting reflection.

There was something in the air that morning. A subtle undercurrent of unease. A whisper threaded through the wind — quiet enough to ignore, strong enough to feel. Even the most hopeful heart could sense it.

Yet for now, they remained steadfast in their roles. They would guard the Land of Soul. They would protect its peace. They would guide those who needed light.

But as the sun climbed higher, warming the world in gold, they understood a deeper truth:

The River of Process was not merely a stream of tranquility. It was a river of transformation.

And transformation, by its very nature, required both light and dark—calm and storm — certainty and surrender.

As Solana, Aurelian, and Seraphiel stood together, they felt the subtle pull of the unknown ahead. They did not yet know what awaited them.

But they knew this:

The journey was about to change them all.

Chapter 2: WHISPERS OF THE LAND

The sun cast its warm light over the Clearing of Soul, its golden rays illuminating the place where the quartet gathered after their journeys across the land. Each had walked a different path through the Land of Soul, and each had returned carrying subtle but undeniable signs of a growing imbalance.

Solana, the Master Healer, arrived first. She knelt in the grass, her fingers brushing the earth with practiced tenderness. Yet the rhythm beneath her touch felt strained, as though the land itself labored to breathe. "The land aches," she murmured, her voice threaded with concern and resolve. "Its pulse is uneven, as if something is disrupting its natural harmony."

A soft rush of wind swept through the clearing as Seraphiel descended from the skies above the Whispering Woods. His luminous wings folded behind him with quiet grace. Even in the light, shadows clung to him in ways they never had before. "The woods are restless," he said, his voice resonant as sunlight breaking through storm clouds. "Their light flickers, dimmed by something unseen."

Aurelian emerged from the direction of the Lumina Mountains, his stride steady but weighted. The mountains had always been a place of strength, yet he carried the tremor of their shifting foundation in his expression. "The peaks tremble," he said, his deep voice steady but grave.

"Their steadfastness is challenged, as though they no longer trust their own roots."

Last to arrive was Zophira, borne on a breeze from the Eternal Sea. Wisdom lived in her gaze — sharp, discerning, unafraid. She paused at the edge of the clearing, her eyes reflecting the turmoil of the tides she had studied. "The sea is clouded," she said, her words cutting cleanly through the air. "Its clarity is muddied by a force that hides beneath the surface."

Together, their observations painted a troubling portrait. The Land of Soul — their sanctuary, their home — was shifting. Even the River of Process, flowing steadily through the clearing, churned with a disquiet that mirrored their own.

Solana rose, brushing the grass from her palms. "Whatever this is," she said, "it touches every corner of our land. The land is calling out for us to heal it."

Seraphiel's wings brightened, though faintly. "But where do we begin? The shadows that linger are not ones we can yet see."

Zophira's gaze sharpened. "We must look within and beyond. Wisdom will guide us, but first, we need the counsel of our people."

Aurelian stepped forward, his presence a steady force. "Then we stand together, as always. The village will help us find our path."

They made their way toward the heart of the village.

The air grew heavier as they approached. The Clearing of Soul, once a place of tranquil gatherings, now carried an undercurrent of tension. Villagers who once moved with purpose now walked with hesitation. Faces that had always been warm and open bore traces of weariness, as though something unseen pressed upon their spirits.

The Council Pavilion rose before them; a circular structure of crystalline stone that shimmered faintly in the waning light. The Elders of Soul sat in a semicircle, their eyes reflecting centuries of wisdom and the weight of the moment.

Elder Myrial, the eldest among them, lifted her hand. Her voice was gentle yet firm, carrying the authority of one who had witnessed countless seasons of change. "You have returned," she said, "but I sense that what you bring is not comfort."

Aurelian bowed his head. "Elder Myrial, the land is changing. The River of Process flows sluggishly in some places and violently in others. The soil hardens. Trees shed their leaves out of season."

Zophira scanned the villagers gathered around the pavilion. "There is a heaviness in the air — not just in the land, but in the hearts of the people. Something unseen presses against us all."

A murmur rippled through the crowd.

Elder Tovrik leaned forward, his expression grave. "We have felt this shift as well. This weight. But we cannot name its cause."

Seraphiel stepped closer, his wings dimming. "The light itself flickers. Something veils the harmony of our land, distorting its essence. This is not a passing disturbance. It is a call to action."

Solana's voice softened, though her words carried urgency. "The people are losing their vitality. Many speak of weariness they cannot explain. Their spirits dim, even when their bodies rest."

Elder Myrial clasped her hands. "If this is true, then the land and its people suffer together. The River of Process reflects our collective state; If it falters, so do we all"

The villagers began to speak, their voices trembling with fear.

"Our crops are withering."

"My child has not smiled in days." "Even the animals are restless."

The Elders exchanged troubled glances.

"You were chosen not only for your gifts," Elder Myrial said, "but for your courage. If the land calls out, you must listen. But this task is not yours alone."

***

Elder Myrial's Memory

Elder Myrial's hands were knotted with years, but when she spoke the room leaned in as if the sound itself were a kind of medicine. She closed her eyes for a moment, letting the memory find its shape, then opened them and began in a voice that was both small and vast.

"There was a winter when the River sang a different song," she said. "I was young then, and the world felt larger because I had not yet learned how small my hands could be. The river's voice changed at dusk — a low, trembling note that made the reeds shiver. People thought it was the wind. We thought it was a storm. But the river was telling us something else."

She paused, and the council listened as if the pause were part of the story. "A family came to the bank that night. Their child had stopped speaking. The parents had tried everything — herbs, songs, and the old turning of the body — but the child's eyes were like closed doors. We brought the child to the River, and we did not ask the river to fix what we could not. We asked it to witness."

Myrial's fingers traced an invisible circle in the air. "We sat in silence until the stars came out. We named the things we feared. We spoke the names of those we had lost and those we still held. The river listened. It did not change the child in a way we could measure. But the child's hand found the mother's, and the mother's hand stopped trembling. The next morning the child spoke a single word — not the word we expected, but a word that meant the child had been seen."

She looked at the quartet, her gaze steady. "The river does not do our work for us. It reflects what we bring. Sometimes the healing is in the naming, sometimes in the tending, sometimes in the willingness to be present without a solution. That is what I remember. That is what I ask of you."

Her story landed like a small stone in the council's pool of worry. It did not erase fear, but it offered a shape for action: witness, name, tend. The villagers shifted, some with tears, some with a slow nod of recognition. Myrial's memory was not a map of answers but a practice — a way to meet the river and the land with hands that knew how to hold.

She gestured to the villagers. "We are a community, bound by the light of Soul. Let us share what we know."

Maelis, a quiet weaver, stepped forward. "My loom resists me. The threads no longer glide. It is as if the fabric of our world is tightening."

Doran, a farmer, added, "The fields feel lifeless. The soil refuses to yield."

One by one, voices rose — a mosaic of subtle but pervasive changes.

Zophira turned to the Elders. "These signs point to a deeper imbalance. We must find its source before it spreads further."

Elder Myrial nodded. "Then you must journey beyond the light of Solara — into the shadows where answers may lie. The Dark Land is not a place we send our own lightly, but it may hold the key to restoring harmony. "

A hush fell over the crowd. The Dark Land was spoken of only in whispers — a realm of Shadows and trials.

Aurelian squared his shoulders. "If the land requires it, we will go. But we will need the strength and blessings of all who remain."

The Elders rose as one, their hands outstretched. "Then it is decided. We will prepare you. But know this: the shadows will test you in ways you cannot yet imagine. To walk the Dark Land is to face not only its terrors, but the darkness within yourselves.

***

Night in the Village Market

The market had emptied but the smell of spices lingered like a memory. Lanterns swung in the breeze, throwing soft, uncertain light across the stalls. Maelis, the weaver, sat on a low stool by her loom, fingers still stained with dye. Her hands moved without thinking, knotting a thread into a pattern she had known since childhood. The loom hummed like a small, steady heart.

A child came up the lane, barefoot and solemn, clutching a scrap of cloth. He stopped when he saw Maelis and tilted his head, the way children do when they are trying to understand something too big for their years. "Aunt Maelis," he said, voice small, "what is a Shadow?"

Maelis looked at him and felt the question like a stone dropped into a still pond. Around them, the village breathed — a dog snoring, a distant argument cut short, the soft clink of a pot. She set her shuttle down and patted the stool beside her. "Come sit," she said.

The child climbed up and folded his legs; the scrap of cloth clutched to his chest. "Is it like the dark?" he asked. "Like when the sun goes away?"

Maelis smiled, not the bright smile of someone who had all the answers, but the kind that makes room for the question. "Sometimes," she said. "But a shadow is also the part of a thing that keeps its shape when the light moves. It's the place where we hide the things we don't want to look at."

The child frowned. "Why would we hide things?"

"Because some things hurt," Maelis said simply. "Or because we think if we hide them, they won't bother anyone. But shadows don't go away just because we don't look. They wait."

He considered this. "Do Shadows ever teach?"

Maelis's fingers found a loose thread, and she began to weave it back into the cloth. "They do," she said. "They teach us what we need to learn. Sometimes they teach us to be brave. Sometimes they teach us to be gentle with ourselves. Sometimes they teach us to ask for help."

The child's eyes widened. "Like when my brother won't say he's scared of the dark?"

"Exactly," Maelis said. "Or like when someone pretends they are fine, but their hands shake when they think no one is watching. Shadows are not always enemies. They are parts of us that need attention."

A man passed by with a basket of wilted herbs and paused when he heard. He dropped a coin into Maelis's palm without looking. "For the boy," he muttered, then kept walking.

The child hugged the scrap of cloth to his chest. "Will the River help?" he asked. "My mother says the River is changing."

Maelis's hands stilled. The loom's hum filled the space between them. "The River listens," she said. "It carries what we give it. But it also asks us to do our part. We must name what we fear, and we must be willing to be seen."

The child's face crumpled a little. "I'm scared my brother will leave."

Maelis's voice softened. "Then tell him. Tell him you're scared. Tell him you love him. Sometimes the thing we fear most is the thing that will bring us closer."

He nodded, small and fierce. "I will."

They sat in companionable silence for a while, the loom's rhythm and the village's night sounds wrapping around them. Maelis thought of the quartet — of Solana's steady hands, Aurelian's guarded jaw, Zophira's sharp eyes, Seraphiel's quiet wings. She thought of the way the land had shifted, the way the River had changed its song. She thought of the small ways people hid their fear: a laugh too loud, a hand that would not meet another's.

When the child rose to go, Maelis pressed a small scrap of woven cloth into his hand. "For your brother," she said. "A thing to remind him that someone sees him."

He hugged her, then ran off into the dark with the scrap fluttering like a small flag. Maelis watched him go, the loom's shuttle moving in her hands. The night felt heavier and softer at once — a place where fear and care lived side by side.

She whispered a line of an old weaving song under her breath, a small prayer for the River and for the people who lived by it.

***

Maelis the Weaver

She stayed a moment longer at her loom, letting the song settle into the threads. She whispered a line of an old weaving song under her breath, a small prayer for the River and for the people who lived by it. The shuttle moved in her hands like a heartbeat; the cloth grew, slow and sure, a small map of the village stitched in indigo and gold.

By the time the lanterns swung low and the market emptied, Maelis had wound a new pattern into the warp — a braid of river lines and small, steady knots meant to hold memory. A neighbor's cat threaded between her feet, and she laughed softly, the sound a bright stitch against the night. The scrap of cloth the child had run off with earlier lay folded on the stool, its colors catching the lamplight like a promise.

A man came by his shoulders hunched with worry and paused at her stall. He did not speak at first; he only set a small bundle of wilted herbs on the table and watched her hands. "My wife says the herbs won't take," he said finally, voice rough with sleeplessness. "The soil won't answer."

Maelis did not look up. Her fingers kept their rhythm. "Sometimes the land asks for a different kind of tending," she said. "Not only water and seed, but a story to hold the work. Tell the soil what you hope for. Sing to it the name of the thing you want to grow." She tied a tiny knot into the edge of the cloth and handed it to him. "Take this. Keep it where you plant. It is only a stitch, but stitches remember."

He blinked, surprised, then accepted the scrap as if it were a talisman. "Will it help?" he asked.

"It will remind you to return," Maelis said. "That is often the work the land needs most."

A child's bare feet padded back into the stall. He held the scrap she had given him earlier, now frayed at the edges from running. "Aunt Maelis," he said, voice small and urgent, "what do you do when the shadow is too big?"

Maelis set the shuttle down and patted the stool beside her. "You make a place for it," she said. "You weave it into something useful. You do not pretend it is not there. You give it a thread and a name, and you keep working." She showed him how to tuck the scrap into a pocket so it would not be lost. "And you tell someone. We do not carry the dark alone."

He nodded, fierce and fragile, and tucked the cloth close. The man with the herbs watched them both, and something like relief softened his face.

When the child left, Maelis returned to her loom. The pattern she wove that night was not a grand design but a small, stubborn thing: a border of tiny jasmines, a line of river knots, a single woven compass in the corner. It was a cloth meant to be given away — a practical blessing for hands that needed to remember they were seen.

She hummed the old song again, softer now. The night felt heavier and softer at once — a place where fear and care lived side by side. She tied off the final thread and folded the cloth, then slipped it into a basket with others she had made for those who might need a reminder: a farmer, a mother, a boy who feared his brother would leave.

Before she closed the stall, Maelis wrote a small note and tucked it into the basket: We weave what we cannot carry alone. She left the lantern low and walked home under the river-silvered sky, the loom's rhythm still in her hands like a promise.

The song was not a cure; it was a way to hold what was fragile. In the morning she would wake and weave again, and the village would wake and speak and barter and worry. Tonight, there was a child running with a scrap of cloth and a man who had dropped a coin without looking. Tonight, there was a small act of seeing.

Despite their fear, the villagers stepped forward — offering provisions, blessings, and silent prayers.

As the sun dipped below the horizon, casting a golden glow over the village, the quartet stood at the center of the gathering, their resolve solidifying.

The journey into the Dark Land would not be taken lightly.

But they would walk it together — for the sake of the Land of Soul, and for all who called it home.

Chapter 3: THE PATH INTO SHADOW

The quartet moved cautiously through the shadowed expanse of the Dark Land, the warmth of the Land of Soul fading behind them like a memory slipping from the edges of the mind. The terrain was jagged and uneven, the air carrying an unnatural chill that clung to their skin. Each breath felt thin, as though the land itself resisted their presence. Mist thickened around them, blurring the line between what was real and what was imagined.

They reached a clearing encircled by ancient, gnarled trees whose branches twisted like grasping hands. The air was still — so still it felt oppressive, as if silence itself pressed against their chests. Then a faint sound broke the quiet: a low, guttural laugh that slithered through the mist.

"Do you feel it yet?" a voice whispered, its tone curling like smoke. "That creeping dread… that sinking weight in your hearts. You should. It's only just begun."

A figure emerged from the shadows, its form shifting and pulsing with malice. Fearmonger. A living embodiment of dread, its presence clawed at the edges of their minds, cold and invasive.

"What is that?" Solana whispered, clutching the vial of water to her chest.

"Fear," Zophira said, her voice steady but her eyes wary. "Given form." Fearmonger's laughter rippled through the clearing, threaded with mockery. "How astute. But what good is wisdom here, Zophira, when

clarity itself is an illusion?"

The shadow surged forward, splitting into tendrils that reached for each of them. Instinctively, the quartet scattered, their gifts igniting in response.

Aurelian summoned a shield of golden light, courage radiating outward to protect the group. "Stay together!" he called, though even his voice trembled beneath the weight of the presence before them.

Fearmonger's tendrils twisted around his shield, cold as winter stone. "Your courage is a cage, Aurelian," the voice hissed inside his mind. "You carry it for others, but when will it break you? When will you collapse beneath the weight of your own expectations?"

Aurelian staggered as the shield flickered. Memories surged —

***

Aurelian's Echo

When the light died in his hands, it was not sudden. It had been a slow unthreading — a series of small loosening things that, together, made a fall. He had learned to carry steadiness like armor: a jaw set against panic, a breath counted twice before action, a hand that steadied others even when it trembled. Tonight, the tremor had been there again, a familiar echo that tasted of iron and old promises.

He crouched on the cracked earth after the shockwave; palms pressed to the stone as if to anchor himself. The ground hummed with the river's distant voice, but beneath that hum was another sound he could not name — the memory's cadence. It came unbidden: the smell of smoke, the sharpness of a broken banner, the weight of a child's small body in his arms.

It had been years, and yet the night returned with the clarity of a wound reopened. The village had been on the edge of a winter storm, roofs thin with frost, and the enemy had come like a rumor turned real. He had stood at the gate with a line of men and women who trusted him because he had never let them see the part of him that doubted. He had given orders, moved people, held the line. He had felt, for a moment, the old certainty — that strength could be enough.

Then the wall cracked.

A plank gave beneath a child's foot. A shout. A scramble. He had reached, fingers closing on a sleeve, and the world had tilted. He remembered the sound of splintering wood like a chorus of small betrayals. He remembered the child's face — not a face of fear but of surprise, as if the child had expected the world to hold him and found it would not. Aurelian had pulled and pulled and then the weight had been gone. The child's body had been lighter than he expected and heavier than his hands could bear.

He had carried that lightness to the healer's tent and watched the breath leave a life like a candle guttering. He had felt the heat of failure spread through him, not as a single blow but as a slow, corrosive certainty: I could not keep them safe. The vow he had made that night — to never let a life slip through his fingers again — had become a chain as much as a promise. He tightened it around himself until it cut.

Now, in the Dark Land, Fearmonger had spoken the truth he had been avoiding; courage could become a cage. The memory rose not to shame him but to teach him the shape of his fear. He pressed his forehead to his knuckles and let the old images come without flinching. The child's laugh, the mother's empty hands, the way the healer had looked at him with a softness that was not pity but a question: How will you live with this?

Aurelian breathed in the cold air and let the present press against the past. He felt Solana's warmth like a hand at his back, Seraphiel's light like a small, steady pulse, Zophira's presence like a compass. They were not the same as the people he had failed, but they were reasons to keep trying. He had to learn the difference between carrying responsibility and carrying the impossible.

He rose slowly, the memory folding into him like a map with a new route marked. He would not erase the night; he would carry it, but differently. Where before the memory had been a stone in his chest, now it could be a marker — a place to stop and remember why he fought, not a weight that made him fall.

He ran his thumb along the scar on his palm, a small, private ritual he had developed after that winter. The scar was a map of a night he could not change; the thumb's motion was a promise to himself that he would not let the past calcify into paralysis. He would stand between the land and its harm, yes, but he would also learn to ask for help when the line blurred. Courage, he told himself, was not only the act of standing; it was the act of letting others stand with you.

When he looked up, the others were gathering themselves, faces set but softer than before. The shield he carried felt less like a cage and more like a tool — imperfect, yes, but useful when wielded with care. He stepped forward, not to prove anything, but because the path required him to move. The memory would remain; it would teach him how to hold, not how to break.

He walked with the slow, deliberate steps of someone who had learned to carry both grief and purpose. The Dark Land would test him again, and he would be tested by his own limits. But for the first time in a long while, the vow in his chest felt like a chosen burden rather than a sentence.

"Stand together!" he shouted, voice cracking through the haze.

Zophira inhaled sharply, her mind clearing. I am not my doubt. Her voice rang out, sharp and steady. "Solana, Seraphiel — focus on your gifts! Fear only has power if we let it!"

Solana gripped the vial, warmth returning to her hands. She released its energy into the air, a glowing mist that wrapped around the group, soothing their minds and pushing back the shadow's influence.

Together, their gifts intertwined — courage, clarity, healing, illumination — braiding through the clearing like a living force. Fearmonger howled, its form splintering as their unity pressed against it.

"This is not over!" it hissed as it dissolved into the shadows.

Silence settled over the clearing, the oppressive weight, lifting.

***

Night After Fearmonger

They made camp in a hollow where the mist thinned enough to see the stars like distant, indifferent eyes. A small fire burned, more for ritual than warmth, its light a fragile circle against the dark. The quartet sat in a loose ring, each tending to small tasks that kept their hands busy and their minds from unspooling.

Solana boiled water and hummed a low, steady tune that seemed to stitch the air. Aurelian sharpened his blade with slow, precise strokes, the metal singing under his hand. Zophira traced patterns in the dirt with a stick, as if mapping the way the land had shifted. Seraphiel sat with wings folded, eyes closed, breathing as if counting the rhythm of the world.

Silence held them for a long time, not empty but full of the things they had not yet said. Finally, Solana broke it, not with words about the battle but with a small, practical question. "Who will watch the eastern pass tomorrow?"

Aurelian looked up, and for a moment the old armor returned. "I will," he said. The answer was automatic, a reflex of duty.

Zophira's stick paused. "You need rest," she said. "You were not yourself out there."

He set the blade down. "Neither were you," he replied, not unkindly. "We all felt it."

Seraphiel opened his eyes and let the light from the fire touch them. "We felt what we carry," he said. "Not just what the Dark Land throws at us."

The words hung between them. Solana's hands were stilling over the kettle. "I keep thinking of the child," she said quietly. "Not the one we lost, but the one I couldn't help long ago. It comes back like a tide."

Aurelian's jaw tightened. "It comes back for me too," he admitted. "I keep seeing the plank break."

Zophira's voice was softer than usual. "I saw a moment when I misread a tide chart and a boat nearly capsized. I could have been wrong and led them into harm."

They each named a small failure, not to punish themselves but to make the weight visible. Naming it made it less monstrous, less a shapeless accusation and more a thing they could look at together.

Seraphiel rose and walked to the edge of the camp, his silhouette a thin line against the mist. He returned with a small sprig of jasmine, its scent a fragile promise of home.

He handed it to Solana. "For remembering," he said.

She accepted it with a nod, pressing the sprig to her lips before tucking it into her robe. "For remembering," she echoed.

Aurelian watched them, the muscles in his face loosening. "We cannot carry everything," he said finally. "But we can carry some things together."

Zophira looked at him, and for the first time that night there was no sharpness in her gaze. "Then let us decide what we will carry and what we will leave for the land to hold," she said. "Not everything is ours to fix."

They sat with that, the fire's light breathing with them. The Dark Land had shown them their edges; the night would teach them how to live with them. Small acts — a shared sprig, a named failure, a watch taken in turns — became the quiet architecture of their endurance.

When sleep finally came, it wasn't deep but a small, necessary rest. They slept in shifts, each waking to the other's breath, each making a quiet promise that they would not face the next test alone.

Chapter 4: ECHOES IN THE MIST

The Dark Land inhaled them and held its breath. Mist pooled in the hollows of the road and rose in slow, deliberate waves, tasting leather and breath and the faint metallic tang of Solana's vial. It moved like a living thing, curious and patient, testing seams and weak stitches where memory might leak through.

Solana kept one hand on the vial as if it were a lifeline. Its warmth was a private certainty against the cold that wanted to unmake edges. She watched the others the way someone watches embers—searching for the first dulling, the first sign that a light might gutter. The question she did not voice sat under her ribs like a small stone.

Aurelian walked at the front, feet setting a steady rhythm into the road. He carried himself like a man who had learned to make promises to the ground; for now, those promises held. When the mist pressed at his face he did not flinch. He breathed through it, letting the cold sharpen his focus. His voice, when he used it, was a measured instrument. He said what needed saying and no more.

Zophira moved with a different kind of steadiness—less show, more calculation. She read the fog the way she read maps, feeling for the subtle folds where the land remembered footsteps. Her fingers twitched as if tracing invisible contours; her eyes catalogued the mist's density like a surveyor. She kept her motions small and precise.

Seraphiel's wings were a dim halo in the gray, light that did not shout but insisted. It pulsed with his breath, brightening when he forced himself to hope and dimming when doubt grazed him. He kept his palms open, as if to catch whatever the mist might throw. He was the first to flinch when the shapes began to resolve.

Shadows gathered like a rumor—edges first, then faces that slid between recognition and blankness, then a ring of them drifting closer with slow, patient hunger. These were not simple phantoms but layered things: Echoes that wore memory like a borrowed coat. Some mimicked voices, some carried smells, some pressed images into the mind like wet paper.

Aurelian halted and raised a hand. The motion was small but precise; it tightened the circle. The nearest Echo leaned forward. Its voice was not a whisper but a staged performance, each syllable shaped to pry open the soft places. **"You promised,"** it intoned, and the word struck Seraphiel like a bell in a hollow room.

The world folded. For a breath the road was not road but ash and tile and the small, terrible geometry of a choice he had made once and could not unmake.

***

Seraphiel's Testament

The courtyard had been a rectangle of ash and broken tile, a place where the sun came through in thin, angry slashes. Smoke braided itself into the rafters; the air tasted of iron and boiled cabbage gone sour. He had been younger then, wings not yet the slow, deliberate thing they were now, and the promise had been a small, bright thing—an oath spoken over a child's fevered brow, a vow to bring water, to find a healer, to keep the weak warm until morning. The child's laugh had been a brittle bell; the elder's cough had been a rhythm he thought he could learn to answer.

He remembered the woman with the cane—her knuckles white with flour, the way she kept patting the pot as if stirring could make the world right again. He remembered the farmer's hands, split and bleeding, the teacher's spectacles bent and useless on a face that still tried to read the sky for meaning. He had moved among them like a man with a list, promising small things he could not yet see how to deliver. Then the wind changed. A roof gave with a sound like a great animal collapsing. A child's kite snagged in a blackened branch and the string burned between his fingers before he understood what was happening.

He had reached for the kite and then for the child and then for the door that led to the storeroom where the elders had been moved, and each reach had been a fraction too late. The smoke filled his mouth; the world narrowed to the heat of a single moment. He had pulled one small body free and left another behind because there was only so much breath to give. The promise—bright, urgent—had folded inward like paper left in rain. The memory did not accuse with words; it showed him the weight of the choice, the exact texture of the rope he had failed to hold. That texture lived in his hands now, a grit under the skin that no light could smooth away.

He staggered; the mist was at his throat again. The Echo's face hovered, a mirror of the child and the elder and the farmer—accusation braided into its features. **"You left them,"** it sang, vowels sharpened into knives. **"You left the small, weak and the old to the dark."**

They moved without the old choreography of speech. Aurelian's hand closed on Seraphiel's shoulder—hard, grounding. Solana's fingers found the vial at her belt and drew it free. Zophira's hands went to the pack and produced a length of braided cord threaded with three tokens: a feather, a sliver of glass, a scrap of woven cloth. They called it the **chord**—a practiced countermeasure: braid, name, bind.

Zophira began the motion without fanfare. Her fingers tied the feather to the cord and, as she worked, a small memory slid into her mind—one she did not speak aloud. She had learned the braid from an old woman who kept a stall at the river market, a woman who mended nets and named the fish she caught so they would not be lost to the current. The woman had taught Zophira that names make things stay put; that a thing with a name is harder to let go. Zophira had practiced the motion with cold hands and a stubborn jaw until the weave felt like a sentence she could say with her fingers. The recollection steadied her hands now.

She whispered a single name into the thread—an anchor. Solana tipped the vial and let a thin bead of warmth spill onto the cloth; the scent of the glow mingled with the mist. Aurelian pressed his palm to the glass sliver until it warmed; the contact was a tether to the present.

The Echo's performance swelled, trying to drown the small, domestic motions. It layered sounds—children's laughter, a lullaby half remembered, the rasp of an old woman's cough—until the air vibrated with possibility. It offered a future like a trap: roads littered with faces they could not save, houses unmade, elders left to the cold. The vision was not only threat; it was a seduction toward despair.

Zophira braided the tokens into the cord with the economy of someone who had done this in worse weather. Each weave was a syllable of resistance. When she finished she held the chord out like a small, human net. **"Name what you fear,"** she said, voice low and precise. The command cut through the Echo's performance.

The Echo answered with a chorus—laughter, a snapped string, a child's cry, the wheeze of an old woman—but the chord thrummed in reply, a thin, stubborn vibration. Seraphiel's throat closed; the memory pushed like a tide. He could have fallen into it, let the past become a place to live again. Instead, he took the chord with hands that trembled and spoke one name—soft, private, the name of the elder he had failed.

Saying the name did not erase the image; it gave the image a place and a voice. Solana pressed the vial to his palm; warmth bled into him, not as a cure but as a steadying. Aurelian's grip tightened on his shoulder. Zophira's braid hummed with the small power of things named and held.

The Echo recoiled as if struck. Its edges frayed; the faces that had been so precise blurred into smoke. It tried to recompose itself into a future vision, but the chord's loop closed around that possibility too—names woven into a human net. The Echo's voice thinned into a brittle question: **"Who will carry the weight?"**

Seraphiel answered without grand speech. He let the name fall again, and this time the sound was not a confession but a promise. The light in his wings steadied, not bright and triumphant but honest and measured. The memory did not vanish; it settled into him like a scar that still needed tending.

The Echo dissolved into a slow rain of ash and whisper. The mist swallowed the last of it, the road exhaled. They did not celebrate. They rearranged themselves—closer, not by ceremony but by a small need of comfort: a hand on a shoulder, a shared warmth, a named thing, looped into a cord.

***

Aftermath

Silence settled like a thin cloth over them. The mist thinned but did not leave; it lingered at the edges like a question. Solana sat on a low stone and cradled the vial, watching the glow pulse faintly beneath her palm. Each pulse cost her something—an ache in the bones, a tremor in the fingers—and she counted the toll in the way the light dimmed a fraction with every breath.

Seraphiel flexed his hands and felt the grit of ash under his nails, a residue that would not wash away with water. He did not speak; he only let the name he had said hang in the air, a small, stubborn fact. Aurelian kept his hand on Seraphiel's shoulder longer than necessary, not to command but to remind the other man that he was not alone in the weight.

Zophira sat a little apart, the chord coiled in her lap. Her eyes were distant, cataloguing the fray in the braid and the way the glass sliver had warmed. She thought of the river woman and the markets and the first time she had tied a name into thread; the memory steadied her now like a practiced knot. She did not speak of it. She only began, with small, careful motions, to reweave the chord's loose end—repairing what had been used, knowing each repair made the cord thinner.

They moved on when they were ready, not because the mist had forgiven them but because the road demanded steps. The cost of the countermeasure sat in their bodies: Solana's hand trembled, Seraphiel's breath came with a small hitch, Zophira's fingers were raw where the braid had rubbed, Aurelian's jaw was tight. None of it was dramatic; it was the slow arithmetic of survival. They carried the names with them, small weights that would shape the next choices they made.

Chapter 5: THE HEART OF THE DARK LAND

The air grew heavier as the quartet pressed deeper into the Dark Land. It was a realm unlike any they had ever encountered, a place where the boundaries between the external and the internal blurred. The terrain seemed alive, shifting and reshaping itself with each step they took. The ground beneath their feet was uneven and treacherous, alternating between hard, cracked jagged stones and patches of slick, black mud.

The light from Seraphiel's wings illuminated their path, but it was faint and flickering, swallowed almost entirely by the oppressive gloom. Around them, the land seemed to pulse, a faint vibration coursing through the air as if the Dark Land itself were breathing.

"This place," Zophira murmured, her voice tinged with awe and unease. "It feels aware."

And it was. The Dark Land was no ordinary realm — it was a mirror of the soul's darkest recesses, a reflection of the fears, doubts, and wounds that lay buried deep within. It was a place that twisted and adapted, responding to the vulnerabilities of those who dared to walk its paths.

None of them said so, but each of them felt it — the subtle, nauseating recognition that the land already knew them. Not in the way a predator knows prey. In the way a mirror knows a face. Every ridge and hollow in the terrain corresponded to something inside them, and the longer they walked, the harder it became to pretend they were only passing through.

Aurelian kept his hand on his shield, but his grip had changed. He was no longer bracing for an external threat. He was holding onto the one thing that still felt like himself — the weight of duty, the shape of protection — because everything else in this place seemed determined to dissolve the boundaries between who he was and what he feared.

The landscape was a patchwork of surreal and disjointed elements. Dead trees with twisted, gnarled branches reached skyward like skeletal hands. Pools of dark, still water dotted the ground, their surfaces unnaturally smooth and reflective, showing distorted images of the quartet's faces when they glanced at them. The sky above was an endless expanse of gray, neither day nor night, with faint streaks of crimson and violet bleeding through the clouds like veins.

Then there was the River of Process, cutting through the heart of the Dark Land like a living artery. Its waters were unlike those in the Land of Soul. Here, the river was darker, its surface rippling with a strange, silvery sheen that reflected the tumult of the land. It churned violently in some places, a raging torrent that carved jagged paths through the stone, while in others, it was eerily still, its surface as smooth as glass. The sound of its flow was haunting — a mix of whispers, cries, and echoes that seemed to come from deep within its depths.

Solana paused at the river's edge; her gaze fixed on the rushing water. "It's the same river," she said, her voice barely above a whisper. "But it feels… different." "It's reflecting this place," Zophira said, kneeling to touch the water's surface. The ripples spread outward, and for a moment, she saw fragments of her own face staring back at her, twisted with doubt and fear. She pulled her hand back quickly, her heart pounding. "It's showing us who we are — what we're struggling with."

Solana had not touched the water. She stood a step behind the others, arms wrapped around herself, and for a long moment no one noticed. That was the part she couldn't say aloud — that in a place built from hidden wounds, her first instinct was still to disappear. To make herself smaller. To watch the others, and tend their feeling, and never once ask what the river was showing her.

But she had seen it. In the half-second before Zophira pulled her hand back, Solana had caught her own reflection in the ripple — not twisted, not frightened. Empty. A version of herself with hands still extended, still reaching, still giving, but with nothing left behind the gesture. A woman shaped entirely by what she poured into others, with no interior of her own.

She tightened her arms around herself and said nothing. But her breathing changed, and Aurelian glanced at her — not with the protective instinct she expected, but with something quieter. Recognition. As though the river had shown him something similar.

Seraphiel stood beside her, his wings dimmed as he stared into the river. "The River of Process doesn't just flow through the Land of Soul," he said, his voice thoughtful. "It flows through the Dark Land as well, because the journey doesn't end with peace. Growth requires struggle. Even here, the river carries us forward, through the chaos."

The group followed the river for a time, its winding path leading them deeper into the heart of the Dark Land. As they walked, the environment around them continued to shift. The air grew colder, and the trees became denser, their branches intertwining overhead to form a canopy that blocked out what little light remained. The ground was littered with fallen leaves that crumbled to ash beneath their feet.

"Do you feel that?" Aurelian asked, his voice low. The others nodded. The atmosphere had changed again, the weight of the land pressing more heavily on their shoulders. The whispers from the river grew louder, mingling with faint echoes that seemed to come from the shadows themselves.

Seraphiel's wings pulled closer to his body, their light reduced to a thin, uncertain glow. He had been illuminating their path since they entered the Dark Land, and for the first time, the effort registered as cost. Not physical exhaustion — something deeper. Each pulse of light felt like an admission: I am afraid of what happens when I stop. The Dark Land pressed against his glow the way deep water presses against a diver's chest, and the question it asked was not whether he could keep shining, but whether he knew who he was without the light.

He didn't answer. Not yet. But the question lodged itself beneath his ribs like a stone, and he carried it forward.

The River of Process, though turbulent, was a constant presence, its flow guiding them even when the path seemed uncertain. At times, the group found themselves walking alongside the river, its dark waters a source of both unease and strange comfort. At other times, they had to cross it, wading through its icy currents or leaping over jagged stones to avoid being swept away.

Each interaction with the river was a reminder of its duality. It was a force of transformation, carrying them through the trials of the Dark Land, but it also reflected their innermost struggles, forcing them to confront the shadows within themselves.

Zophira broke the silence first, though her voice was smaller than usual. "I keep trying to map this place," she said. "The terrain, the river patterns, the distances between landmarks. I keep trying to find the logic." She paused, and when she spoke again, the admission cost her something visible — her jaw tightened, her eyes dropped. "There is no logic. And I don't know how to move through a place I can't understand."

It was the most vulnerable thing she had said since they entered the Dark Land. Aurelian looked at her, and instead of offering reassurance — the thing he would have done an hour ago, the shield-response, the protective reflex — he simply nodded. "I don't either," he said. And the honesty of it settled between them like a shared breath.

As they continued, the river led them to a clearing where the ground was smoother, the air quieter. In the center of the clearing stood a single, massive tree — its bark blackened and scarred, its branches reaching upward like twisted arms. At its base, the river pooled into a small, still pond, its surface reflecting the tree in perfect detail.

"This feels like a crossroads," Zophira said, her voice thoughtful. "The river is guiding us, but it's also asking us to choose. Do we continue forward, deeper into the shadows? Or do we stop here, safe from whatever lies ahead?"

Solana finally spoke, and her voice carried something none of them had heard before — not the steady warmth of the healer, but the unsteady truth of a woman standing at her own edge.

"I'm afraid," she said. Not to anyone in particular. To the tree. To the river. To the version of herself she had seen in the water. "Not of what's ahead. I'm afraid that I've been so busy tending everyone else that I don't know what I look like when I'm not giving something away."

The silence that followed was not uncomfortable. It was the kind of silence that happens when someone says the thing everyone has been thinking. Seraphiel's wings brightened — not in response to danger, but in response to truth. As though honesty itself was a kind of light the Dark Land could not swallow.

Aurelian stepped forward, his gaze fixed on the tree. "Stopping isn't an option. We've come this far, and the Land of Soul is depending on us."

The others nodded, their resolve firm despite the weight of the land pressing against them. The tree loomed above them as they crossed the clearing, its presence a silent witness to their journey. The River of Process continued its flow, carving its path through the Dark Land as it carried them forward into the unknown.

The Dark Land was alive, ever-changing, and relentless. But so were they. And with every step, they grew stronger, more attuned to the challenges that lay ahead. The shadows might test them, but the river reminded them that even in the darkest places, there was movement, transformation, and the promise of light.

Chapter 6: THE SHADOWKEEPER

The path ahead narrowed, forcing the quartet to tread carefully as they followed the winding River of Process deeper into the Dark Land. The oppressive air thickened around them, not just with mist but with something intangible — a presence that seemed to grow stronger with every step they took.

The river, their constant companion, now churned violently beside them, its waters reflecting not the world around them but flashes of memories — fragments of their pasts. Aurelian saw glimpses of battles he had fought, moments when his courage had faltered. Solana caught the faint outline of faces she had healed but could no longer name. Seraphiel saw himself standing alone, his wings dimmed, as the weight of failure bore down on him. And Zophira saw the countless decisions she had made, each one branching into paths she could no longer walk.

"This place… it's pulling at something," Zophira murmured, her voice heavy with the weight of realization. "Not just our fears, but our pasts."

The group pressed on, the path widening to reveal a barren expanse. In its center stood a massive, crumbling archway, blackened with age. It loomed over them; its surface etched with symbols they couldn't decipher. Beyond it, the mist seemed darker, heavier, as if it were guarding something.

"We're being led," Seraphiel said, his wings flexing uneasily. "But to what?"

As if in answer, the air grew colder, and a low, resonant voice echoed through the clearing. "You who walk the river's edge, do you carry the weight of what came before?"

The quartet froze, their eyes scanning the shadows. From beneath the archway emerged a figure cloaked in darkness, its form both solid and insubstantial. Its face was hidden, but its eyes burned with an eerie, otherworldly light. This was no ordinary shadow. This was Shadowkeeper — the embodiment of past mistakes, regrets, and failures that bound the soul.

Shadowkeeper's presence was overwhelming, its voice reverberating in their minds. "Every step you take is weighed by the burden of what lies behind you. Do you think you can move forward without facing it?"

Aurelian stepped forward, his courage flaring. "We've come to face whatever lies ahead, even you."

Shadowkeeper tilted its head; its voice laced with both curiosity and challenge. "And what of what lies behind? Do you not see? Your past clings to you, a shadow woven into your very being. You carry it with you, and yet you pretend it does not exist."

The ground beneath them shifted, and the River of Process surged violently, its waters rising to form mirrored walls around the quartet. Each wall reflected a moment from their past, distorted and magnified. The reflections rippled with emotion, drawing them into the memories they had tried to bury.

Aurelian saw himself standing over a battlefield, his hands bloodied, his shoulders bowed under the weight of failure. The faces of those he had failed to protect stared back at him, their eyes filled with accusation. His breath hitched as Shadowkeeper's voice cut through the scene. "Courage cannot erase failure, Aurelian. It only carries it forward. Will you let it define you?"

Zophira's reflection showed her standing alone in a room filled with maps and books, her hands trembling as she made a choice that rippled through countless lives. She saw the faces of those who had suffered because of her decisions, and the weight of responsibility pressed down on her. “Wisdom is not infallible, Zophira,” Shadowkeeper whispered. “Can you accept that even clarity falters?”

Solana’s mirrored image was surrounded by those she had healed, their faces turning to ash as they reached for her. She saw herself giving and giving, her own body withering with each touch. “You cannot heal what is already gone,” the Shadow Keeper said, its voice softer now. “Will you learn to heal yourself?”

Seraphiel’s wings were dimmed in his reflection, his light extinguished as he stood alone in the dark. He saw himself trying to guide others, only for them to fall, their faith in him broken. “Light bearer,” Shadowkeeper said, its tone piercing, “what becomes of the light when it fails? Can you bear to carry it still?”

The quartet stood in silence, each grappling with the weight of what they saw. Shadowkeeper stepped closer, its form towering over them. “You cannot outrun your past,” it said. “It is part of you, woven into the fabric of

your soul. But you must decide will it bind you, or will it become the foundation upon which you rise?”

Zophira was the first to speak, her voice steady despite the tremor in her hands. “The past… it is not a prison. It is a lesson. Every mistake, every regret, every failure — it has shaped me, but it does not define me.”

Her words seemed to ripple through the group, igniting something within them. Solana stepped forward, her voice soft but firm. “I’ve given so much of myself to others, but I see now that I cannot heal without first honoring my own spirit. The past is not a wound — it is a part of the healing.”

Aurelian clenched his fists, his courage flaring anew. “I’ve failed, yes. But failure doesn’t mean I stop trying. Courage isn’t about being unbroken

— it’s about rising, even when you are.”

Seraphiel unfurled his wings, their light burning brighter than before. “My light is not perfect. It falters, it dims, but it endures. He felt the old ache behind his ribs—familiar and exact. . The past does not extinguish it — it fuels it.”

Shadowkeeper regarded them silently for a long moment before stepping back. The mirrored walls dissolved, and the River of Process returned to its normal flow. The Keeper's voice was softer now, almost reverent. "You have faced what many cannot. The past is a burden, yes, but it is also a gift. Carry it wisely."

Shadowkeeper faded into the mist, leaving the quartet standing in the clearing. The air felt lighter, and the river's whispers grew softer, more harmonious.

The group pressed on, their steps more certain, the River of Process guiding them forward. The Dark Land still loomed around them, but they carried something new within them — a deeper understanding of themselves, forged in the crucible of their pasts.

Chapter 7: THE WRATHBEARER

The Dark Land shifted as the quartet pressed deeper, its terrain jagged and restless. The River of Process churned beside them — no longer whispering, but groaning, heavy with heat. The air itself felt fevered.

"Does anyone else feel that?" Solana murmured, touching her chest. "Like the land is burning from the inside?"

Aurelian nodded. "Something is rising."

The heat intensified, curling through the air in sharp, dry gusts. The mist peeled back, replaced by shimmering waves that distorted the ground. The earth beneath their feet reverberated slowly at first, then faster, like a furious heartbeat buried beneath stone.

A roar erupted.

Fire surged upward, twisting into the shape of a figure taller than any they had faced. Its form was a molten silhouette — jagged, pulsing, shifting from flame to shadow and back again. The air crackled around it, each spark sounding like a snapped bone.

***

The Wrathbearer.

Its voice scraped through the air like metal dragged across stone.

"So, the four of you walk willingly into flame."

Its head tilted, ember eyes narrowing. "Tell me — do you believe your light can survive fire?"

Aurelian stepped forward, instinctively positioning himself between the

creature and his companions. "We don't fear you."

A low, vibrating laugh rolled through the heat. "You don't fear me," it said. "You fear the fire you carry."

A flame-laced claw pointed at Aurelian.

"You swallow it. Smother it. And pretend that makes you strong."

Aurelian stiffened, saying nothing.

The Wrathbearer advanced. "Strength without expression becomes pressure. Pressure becomes fire. Fire — when denied — burns everything." Zophira drew in a sharp breath. "It's more than anger."

"Yes," the Wrathbearer hissed. "I am the truth of what you hide when you pretend to be wise. When you pretend to know."

Zophira flinched — not from heat, but from recognition. The flames swirled around Solana next.. "You," it whispered, and its voice softened cruelly. "Little healer. So gentle. So, giving."

The fire leaned closer. "Tell me — when you tend to everyone else, where does your own rage go? Do you bury it in your bones? Do you pretend it isn't there?"

Solana's grip tightened around her vial, her knuckles paling.

The heat intensified around Seraphiel last, licking at the edges of his wings.

"And you, light-bearer. You shine so brightly, hoping no one sees the fury in your shadows."

Seraphiel inhaled sharply. His wings dimmed at the edges.

The Wrathbearer lifted its arms, and the ground cracked open, flames rising like serpents. "I am not here to destroy you," it thundered. "I am here because you are destroying yourselves."

The land trembled.

The quartet was swallowed in a ring of fire — bright, violent, and suffocating.

Their gifts flickered.

The heat pressed against their chests like clenched fists.

Aurelian staggered first. His voice strained. "I don't… want to hurt anyone."

"You already do," the Wrathbearer said. "Every time you pretend, you're unaffected. Every time you swallow your own truth to protect someone else."

Aurelian trembled — his courage flickering like a candle fighting wind.

Zophira fell to her knees next, gripping the earth. Her clarity blurred as the fire distorted her vision.

"What if my anger blinds me?" she whispered. "What if I speak from pain instead of wisdom?"

"Because you are human," the Wrathbearer growled. "Because you feel.

Your anger is not your enemy — it is your compass."

Solana lifted her vial toward the flames, but heat surged back, pushing her arm down. "I can't lose control," she whispered.

"You cannot heal with a closed heart," the Wrathbearer said. "And your heart is locked behind walls built from your own resentment."

Solana gasped, tears forming instantly and evaporating from the heat. Seraphiel's wings burned at the edges.

"I am not angry," he said, voice trembling. The Wrathbearer towered over him. "Liar."

A burst of flame shot upward, illuminating a dark, fractured reflection of Seraphiel — eyes fierce, jaw clenched, wings damaged.

Seraphiel stared at the image, breath shallow. "What… is that?"

"The part of you that demanded the world be kinder," the Wrathbearer said. "The fury you felt when it wasn't."

Seraphiel's wings dimmed.

"I was never allowed to feel that."

"And yet it lives in you," the Wrathbearer said gently. "Calling for air."

Silence.

No one moved.

Then Zophira's voice broke — soft, shaking, but clear.

"I think… it's not here to punish us. It's here to show us what we deny."

Aurelian lifted his head. "Then we stop denying."

Solana wiped her cheeks, inhaling a tremor. "We allow ourselves to feel."

Seraphiel closed his eyes, wings softening. "We acknowledge our fire… without letting it consume us."

Aurelian stepped forward, meeting the Wrathbearer's ember gaze. "My anger isn't weakness. It's warning. It tells me where I care."

Zophira rose beside him. "My anger isn't failure. It's a signal I need clarity."

Solana's voice steadied. "My anger isn't selfish. It shows where I've ignored my own needs."

Seraphiel unfurled his wings fully — bright, luminous, unwavering.

"My anger isn't darkness. It's passion longing for direction."

The Wrathbearer fell silent.

The flames surrounding the quartet calmed, then lowered. Its molten form softened, flickering like a dying star.

"You have understood," it whispered. "Fire burns. Fire cleanses. Fire transforms. But fire only destroys when denied."

The creature dimmed.; "Carry your flames with honesty," it said, voice fading. "And the land

will burn with renewal — not ruin."

The fire extinguished in a single, soft exhale. The heat dissipated.

The air cooled.

And for the first time since entering the Dark Land… the quartet stood

taller, breathing easier.

Aurelian placed a hand over his heart. "I thought fire was danger. But maybe… it's part of my strength."

Zophira exhaled. "Part of all our strength."

Solana lifted her vial with a steadier hand. "Anger doesn't make us unkind. It makes us honest."

Seraphiel's wings illuminated the path ahead. "Then let us walk in truth.

Flame and all." They made no ceremony of it. Solana knelt and ran cool water over a shallow burn on Aurelian's palm, the motion precise and unhurried; she hummed a single, steady note that steadied both of them. Zophira sat with a scrap of thread and restitched the braid's frayed end, her hands moving like a metronome—each stitch a decision to keep attention where it belonged. Seraphiel folded a scrap of cloth and tucked a name into it, not to hide the memory but to carry it with care. Aurelian flexed his fingers and let the heat's lesson settle into his bones: anger named becomes direction. They did not celebrate. They tended, and in the tending the lesson took root.

They stepped forward. And the land followed.

Chapter 8: SHADOWS OVER SOUL

The Land of Soul, once a sanctuary of harmony and light, now simmered with unrest. The golden glow that had always bathed the village was dimmer, the air thick with unease. The people moved through their days with hesitation, their once-bright faces now etched with tension. It was as if the very essence of their land had begun to fracture, mirroring the unrest within their hearts.

In the Council Pavilion, the Elders gathered, their voices rising in an attempt to quell the discontent spreading through the village.

"This division cannot continue," Elder Myrial said, her voice calm yet strained. "If we allow fear and anger to take hold, we risk losing everything we have built."

But even she felt the weight of the shadows creeping into her thoughts. What if we fail? What if the peace we've maintained was always fragile, destined to shatter under pressure?

Beyond the pavilion, the village square was a cacophony of raised voices. Groups of villagers stood in tense clusters, their words sharp and accusing.

"It's your fault!" shouted Doran, the farmer, his face flushed with anger. "You were the one who insisted on changing the planting cycles. Now the fields are barren, and we're all suffering!"

Maelis, the weaver, snapped back, her hands trembling as she spoke. "And you think I wanted this? I was trying to help! Maybe if you hadn't been so stubborn, we wouldn't be in this mess!"

Their argument drew a crowd, the tension spreading like wildfire. Others began to join in, their voices carrying accusations rooted in old grievances.

"You never cared about anyone but yourself, Doran! We all remember how you hoarded supplies during the last drought!"

"And you, Maelis! Always so quick to judge everyone else — but what have you done to help lately?"

The anger was palpable, each accusation pulling at the buried guilt and resentment the villagers had long ignored. Fear fueled their words — fear of the changes in their land, of the unknown dangers creeping closer, of their own inadequacies. It was easier to lash out than to face the shadows within.

The market smelled of iron and stew; lanterns swung low over stalls where hands—callused, stained, steady—moved with the economy of people who had to make a living. A woman at the fish stall tied a knot and retied it, again and again, as if the rope might remember how to hold. A man who had once been the village's best boatwright stood with his back to the river, his hands empty of tools.

Selene pushed through the press, palms steady as she steadied the fishmen's shaking hands. "Hold the basket," she said, not to soothe but to act. The man's fingers closed around the rope, knuckles white. He did not look up. Later, when the lanterns were dim and the market quieted, he would sit on the riverbank and try to name the fear lodged in his chest. For now, he tied the knot again, and the knot held.

Two women argued over seed allotments at the grain stall, voices low and sharp. A ledger lay open on the table; the miller's handwriting cramped with worry. When the argument threatened to flare, Elder Myrial stepped between them and did not offer a speech. She took the ledger, ran her finger down the list, and marked a line with a steady hand: two extra measures for the north field — watch rotation assigned. The action was small and practical; it shifted the argument into work.

Inside the pavilion, the Elders struggled to maintain order. Elder Tovrik, known for his practicality, slammed his hand on the table. "We must address this now. The people need guidance, not chaos."

"But how can we guide them when we feel it as well?" Elder Lirien countered, her voice trembling. "I've felt the pull of the Shadows myself — the doubts, the anger. It's in all of us."

Myrial closed her eyes, taking a deep breath. She had always been the pillar of knowledge, but even she felt cracks forming within her. The Shadows whispered to her in quiet moments, amplifying her fears. I am not strong enough to hold them together. Maybe I am part of the problem.

Outside, the arguments escalated. Villagers began to dredge up old wounds, blaming one another for past mistakes. Accusations flew, cutting deeper than intended.

"You think we've forgotten how you abandoned us during the flood, Arel? You only saved your own family while the rest of us struggled!"

"And what about you, Nara? You talk about unity, but you've always looked down on us farmers. Don't think we haven't noticed!"

The Elders stepped into the square, their presence commanding enough to quiet the crowd for a moment. Myrial raised her hands, her voice steady despite the turmoil. "Enough! This division will destroy us if we let it. The Shadows are feeding on our fear and anger. We must remember who we are — a community, bound by light and unity."

But her words, though wise, did little to quell the unrest. The Shadows destructive ability had taken root too deeply, whispering doubts into the hearts of the villagers.

"Easy for you to say," someone muttered. "You sit in the pavilion while the rest of us struggle."

Another voice rose in agreement. "What have the Elders done for us lately? Maybe it's time we took matters into our own hands." The words stung, and Myrial felt her resolve waver. She glanced at her fellow Elders, seeing the same doubts mirrored in their faces. The pull of the shadows was stronger than ever, threatening to unravel the fragile unity of the village.

In a quiet corner of the square, a young woman named Lyra knelt beside an elderly villager who had fallen ill. Her hands trembled as she tried to soothe him, her heart heavy with guilt. I can't help him. I'll fail, just like I failed my family during the last crisis.

The guilt was a thread that connected them all — each villager carrying their own burdens, their own unspoken regrets. The Shadows, fueled by the disparity of the people, thrived; weaving a tapestry of division and despair.

As the day wore on, the arguments continued, the air thick with tension. The Elders retreated to the pavilion, their voices low as they tried to devise a solution.

"We need the quartet to return," Lirien said, her voice breaking. "They are the only ones who can restore balance."

"But what if they don't succeed?" Tovrik asked, voicing the fear they all felt. "What if the shadows overpower them?"

Myrial looked out at the village, her heart heavy. She didn't have an answer. All she could do was hope that the quartet would find a way to dispel the darkness, and that the people of Soul could find the light within once more.

As night fell, the village grew quiet, but the unrest remained, simmering beneath the surface. The Elders watched from the pavilion, their thoughts heavy with doubt. The Land of Soul, once a beacon of peace, was now a mirror of the turmoil in its people.

And the Shadows were waiting, ready to consume them all if they gave up.

Chapter 9: HOLLOWSHADE

The mist in the Dark Land thickened as the quartet continued their journey, the oppressive air weighing heavily on their spirits. The River of Process, their constant companion, flowed sluggishly beside them. Its dark waters seemed calmer than before, but the calm was unsettling, as though the river itself had grown tired of its turbulence.

The group moved cautiously, their senses attuned to the eerie silence that enveloped them. Even the usual whispers of the river had faded, leaving only an emptiness that seemed to seep into their very beings.

"This quiet," Seraphiel murmured, his wings flickering faintly in the dim light. "It doesn't feel like peace. It feels… hollow."

The others nodded in silent agreement, their unease growing with each step. The landscape around them was barren, the ground cracked and dry, as if life itself had been drained from it. Dead trees dotted the horizon, their twisted branches reaching skyward like skeletal hands.

As they reached a wide, desolate plain, the air grew colder, and a figure emerged from the shadows. Its form was ghostly and insubstantial, a pale silhouette that seemed to flicker like a dying ember. Its presence was not as overwhelming as the Wrathbearer's fiery rage or the Shadow Keeper's commanding aura, but it was no less suffocating.

This was Hollowshade, the embodiment of apathy and emotional numbness.

Its voice was a low, monotonous whisper that seemed to echo within their minds. "Why do you struggle?" it asked, its words slow and deliberate. "Why do you fight, when nothing truly matters?"

The quartet froze, the weight of Hollowshade's presence pressing down on them. It wasn't a violent force, but a quiet, insidious one that sapped their will to move, to speak, to think.

It was nothing like the Wrathbearer's fire or the Shadowkeeper's commanding weight. Those shadows had demanded something — resistance, reckoning, engagement. Hollowshade demanded nothing. And that was worse. The absence of demand left them standing in the middle of themselves with no enemy to face, no wound to tend, no question to answer. Just silence, stretching in every direction like a landscape with no horizon.

"Keep your guard up," Aurelian said, his voice firm but quieter than usual. "This is another test."

Hollowshade tilted its head, its form flickering slightly. "A test? Is that what you think this is? No. This is truth. The truth you refuse to see. All your struggles, your sacrifices — they are meaningless. They change nothing." The words were like a chilled wind, cutting through their resolve. The quartet exchanged uneasy glances, each of them feeling the pull of Hollowshade's apathy in their own way.

Aurelian felt his courage falter, the strength he prided himself on fading into doubt. What's the point of fighting if it never truly ends? What if all my efforts are for nothing?

His shield arm dropped to his side — not from exhaustion, but from something far more dangerous. Indifference. For a man who had built his identity around standing between others and harm, the absence of urgency felt like a door opening onto a vast, empty field. No one to protect. No threat to brace against. Just the terrifying freedom of not caring. And somewhere beneath the horror of that freedom, a whisper he could barely admit to hearing: What if this is easier? What if I could just set it all down?

His knees didn't buckle. They simply stopped locking. He swayed where he stood, and for the first time in his life, Aurelian did not correct his stance.

Zophira, usually the voice of clarity and reason, found her thoughts clouded. What if there is no path forward? What if my wisdom is just a futile attempt to make sense of chaos?

The maps in her mind — the ones she carried everywhere, the ones she redrew with every new variable — went blank. Not erased. Just irrelevant. She had always feared being wrong. She had never imagined how seductive it would feel to stop trying to be right. The relief was immediate and enormous, like setting down a pack she hadn't realized was crushing her spine. No patterns to track. No paths to calculate. No responsibility for the direction they walked.

She could feel her thoughts slowing, each one arriving later than the last, and the spaces between them filling with a gray, cottony stillness that asked nothing of her. Her fingers, usually restless with notation and measurement, went limp at her sides.

Solana's hands trembled as she clutched the vial of water, its warmth barely noticeable against the cold creeping into her heart. What if healing doesn't matter? What if all I've done has been for a world that cannot be saved?

The vial's warmth faded against her palm, and she let it. That was the part that frightened her most — not the cold, but how good it felt to stop generating heat. She had poured herself into every cracked vessel, every broken body, every grieving heart she had ever touched. She had given until her hands ached and her own pulse felt borrowed. And now Hollowshade was offering her the one thing no one else ever had: permission to stop.

Not permission to rest — she knew the difference. Rest was temporary, a pause before returning. This was permanent. A door that locked behind you. And the relief flooding through her was so immediate, so total, that she understood with sudden clarity why apathy was the most dangerous shadow of all. It didn't attack. It comforted. It wrapped itself around exhaustion and called itself mercy.

Seraphiel's light dimmed, his wings drooping as Hollowshade's words echoed in his mind. What if my light is only a fleeting flicker in endless darkness? Why should I keep trying to shine when it always fades?

His wings folded inward — not the tight, protective fold of hiding, but a slow, settling collapse, like candle wax pooling at the base of a wick. The light had always cost him something. Every glow, every flare, every moment of illumination pulled from a reserve he had never learned to replenish. And now, in Hollowshade's presence, the prospect of dimming felt less like failure and more like homecoming.

No one watching. No one needing his brightness to navigate by. No one measuring their hope against his glow. He could be dark. He could be invisible. He could exist without performing existence, and the land would not notice, and the sky would not fall, and the silence would hold him the way his light never had — without expectation, without cost.

He felt his eyes closing. Not in sleep. In surrender to the oldest exhaustion he carried: the weariness of being seen.

Hollowshade drifted closer, its form expanding to encompass them. "You see?" it whispered. "The shadows are not your enemy. They are your truth. Surrender to the emptiness, and you will find peace."

The group stood frozen, their will drained by the shadow's presence. The silence stretched on, oppressive and unbroken, until Solana's voice, though faint, cut through the stillness.

The word cost her something physical. She felt it tear loose from somewhere below her ribs — a small, stubborn ember that Hollowshade's cold had not quite reached. Her voice cracked on the syllable, and her hands shook, and the effort of speaking against the numbness was like pushing through water that had frozen around her while she stood still.

"No," she said, her tone shaky but resolute. "This… this is not peace.

This is surrender. And I refuse to surrender."

Her words seemed to ignite something in the others.

Not immediately — not the way fire catches kindling. More the way dawn arrives, slow, uncertain, the darkness retreating in increments so small you couldn't point to the moment it began. Aurelian's knees locked again. He felt the click of it in his joints, and with it, a surge of something that was not quite courage but was close enough — the refusal to be comfortable in his own absence.

Aurelian straightened, his courage flaring. "We've faced worse than this. I won't let some shadow tell me my efforts don't matter."

Zophira's eyes cleared as she took a steady breath. "Meaning isn't something we find — it's something we create. Even in the darkest moments, we choose to move forward."

Seraphiel's wings flared with light, their glow piercing through the shadow's encroaching form. "My light is not meaningless. It exists because I choose to make it so."

Hollowshade hissed, its form wavering as the quartet's resolve strengthened. "You think your defiance will change anything? The emptiness will always return. It is inevitable." "Maybe it will," Aurelian said, his voice steady. "But we'll rise again, every time."

The quartet stood together, their gifts combining in a burst of light that pushed Hollowshade back. The shadow writhed, its form dissolved into the mist as it let out a final, low whisper.

"The emptiness is within you. It always will be."

As Hollowshade faded, the oppressive air lifted, and the River of Process began to flow more steadily. The group stood in silence for a moment, each of them grappling with the lingering weight of the encounter. Finally, Zophira spoke. "Hollowshade was right about one thing. The emptiness is within us. But it doesn't define us. What we choose to do with it — that's what matters."

The others nodded, their resolve renewed. The Dark Land was relentless, but so were they. Together, they pressed on, the River of Process guiding them deeper into the unknown.

Chapter 10: SHATTERED PATHS

The landscape shifted beneath their feet, cracking like thin ice under too much weight. The River of Process, once a steady companion, had grown strangely quiet — its whispers muted, its flow sluggish, as though exhausted by the journey.

Zophira paused first, sensing the disturbance before the others.

"Something's wrong," she murmured. "The land feels… severed."

Seraphiel's wings dimmed as he scanned the horizon. "It's more than silence. There's no direction. No pull. As if the land has forgotten where it leads."

Ahead, the path fractured into dozens of splintered trails — branching, twisting, weaving away into the gray horizon. None felt warm. None felt true.

Aurelian frowned, stepping forward cautiously. "The land shouldn't do this. It always guides."

But the paths continued to split, each one dissolving into a haze of uncertainty.

Solana knelt beside the riverbank, dipping her fingers into the still water. Even the liquid felt different — cool, distant, unresponsive.

"It's like the river is numb," she whispered. "Like it can't feel us anymore."

A soft vibration rippled through the air — low, hollow, unsettling.

Then the mist ahead thickened and congealed, pulling together into a vast, dark shape. It was featureless, an absence given form. The temperature dropped as a void-born presence drifted toward them.

A deep, empty voice spoke — flat, emotionless. "Why do you continue?"

The quartet stiffened.

From the mist emerged the Apathetic Void, a mass of unmoving shadow that absorbed the light around it.

"There is no meaning," the Void murmured. "No purpose. Every step you take dissolves into nothing. Why fight a battle already lost?"

The words pulled at their spirits like heavy chains. Before the quartet could respond, a second figure spiraled out of the mist — this one quick, erratic, constantly shifting form and color like a restless dream. Its laughter was sharp and disorienting.

"And if you do keep walking…" it said, voice lilting and mocking, "how will you know which way? Thousands of paths. No certainty. No truth." It twirled in a dizzying arc.

"What if each step takes you further from yourselves?"

***

Perplexia.

The two shadows moved in tandem — stillness and chaos, emptiness and overwhelm. Their combined presence fractured the air around the quartet, making it hard to think, hard to breathe, hard to feel.

Aurelian felt his courage flicker.

"What if… they're right?"

The words tasted foreign on his tongue.

"What if all this — everything — changes nothing?"

Zophira pressed her fingers to her temples as Perplexia's shifting form swirled around her, clouding her thoughts.

"What if I misread every sign?" she whispered. "What if I've led us wrong since the beginning?"

Solana's vial dimmed in her hand.

"What if healing doesn't matter? What if no amount of light can reach what's broken?"

Seraphiel's wings sagged, their glow nearly gone. "What if my light was never meant to last?"

The Void loomed closer, its presence draining their spirits like water seeping from a cracked vessel.

"There is nothing ahead," it said simply. "Nothing to achieve. Nothing to become. Sink into stillness. Let meaning fade."

Perplexia shrieked with erratic laughter. "Or keep going! Take one path, take all of them! Lose yourselves in the maze! Either way, you'll never know if any choice was real."

The ground shuddered.

The dozens of paths multiplied — splitting again, branching like veins of shattered glass.

They stretched endlessly in every direction, each one unfamiliar, each one equally hollow

The quartet stood surrounded by infinite uncertainty.

Aurelian staggered as the weight of indecision pressed into his chest.

"I… I don't know which way to go."

Zophira stared at her hands, shaken. "I can't see anything clearly.

Everything is clouded."

Solana sank to her knees, the numbness creeping through her limbs. "If nothing matters… why try?"

Seraphiel closed his eyes, wings dimmed to the faintest shadow. "What if purpose is just… illusion?"

The Shadows circled them — one smothering, one disorienting —

slowly unraveling their unity.

And then—

A sound broke through the haze. A breath.

Steady. Intentional. Solana lifted her head.

"I… remember something," she whispered. "The river. It taught us this: movement isn't about knowing. It's about choosing."

Zophira blinked, a spark of clarity igniting. "Uncertainty isn't failure.

It's freedom. Paths only form when walked."

Aurelian drew a slow breath, feeling strength return to his chest. "And meaning doesn't exist on its own. We create it."

Seraphiel opened his eyes, wings brightening. "And my light shines because I choose to shine it — not because the world guarantees me a direction."

The Void paused — a faint ripple spreading through its stillness. Perplexia stopped mid-spin, startled.

Solana rose slowly, placing her hand over her heart. "I may not know every step. But I can take the next one."

Zophira nodded, voice steady. "We don't need the whole path to see the first step."

Aurelian stood tall, grounding himself. "Purpose isn't something we find — it's something we live."

Seraphiel's wings unfurled fully, casting illumination across the fracturing landscape. "And meaning grows with us, not ahead of us."

The ground responded. Cracked paths began to merge — slowly, deliberately — like scattered pieces remembering they belonged to a whole. The shattered patterns softened until a single, steady trail emerged before them.

The Void recoiled. "You… reject stillness?"

Aurelian answered, voice firm. "We reject surrender."

Perplexia sputtered, its form fracturing. "And confusion? You reject confusion?"

Zophira shook her head. "No. We embrace uncertainty. We simply refuse to be lost in it."

Light spread across the path, gentle but unwavering.

Solana smiled softly. "One step. One breath. One truth at a time."

Seraphiel's wings glowed brilliantly. "We walk not because we know — but because we choose."

The two Shadows dissolved — one fading into still air, the other shattering into harmless motes of color.

The path ahead solidified.

The quartet stepped forward together, stronger than before.

The River of Process surged quietly beside them — its stillness broken, its flow renewed.

Chapter 11: BREATH IN THE SHADOWS

The quartet found a small clearing along the River of Process. Its sluggish current seemed to carry the same weight they did; slow, reluctant, burdened. The air was still, almost watchful, as if the Dark Land had paused to study them. They settled with space between their bodies, each retreating inward, the day's choices and costs pressing down in the quiet.

Aurelian sat on a jagged rock, hands braced on his knees, staring toward the darkened horizon. His breath stayed measured, disciplined, but his chest refused to loosen. The tension held like a fist he couldn't unclench.

***

Private Confession

They sat apart from the others where the reeds thinned, and the river's voice softened into a steady hush. Aurelian had his back to the water; shoulders squared in that way that made him feel like a wall. Solana sat beside him with her knees drawn up, a small bundle of herbs in her lap held like something living, something that needed gentleness.

For a long time neither spoke. The night held them with patient pressure, as if it were waiting to see which of them would finally tell the truth first.

Solana turned toward him. Lamplight caught the line of her jaw; the tiredness there had nothing to do with sleep. "There's something I haven't told you," she said, careful as a hand over a wound.

Aurelian's fingers stilled against his knee. "What is it?"

She swallowed. "When I was younger, there was a fever. A child in my care." Her grip tightened around the herbs until the leaves whispered. "I did everything I knew; poultices, songs, turning the body and still the child died." Her voice thinned, but it didn't break. "I promised myself I would never let a name fade. I promised I would carry them so others wouldn't have to." She exhaled, the confession finally finding its shape. "But sometimes I think I carried the promise more than the person. I kept the practice and lost the presence."

Aurelian listened without reaching for armor. When he spoke, his voice was softer than she'd heard in a long while. "You carry more than you should," he said. "You make yourself a vessel, then punish yourself for leaking."

She let out a laugh that was almost a sob. "I thought if I held enough names, I could keep the world from losing anyone else." Her eyes stayed on the herbs, as if they could absorb what she couldn't. "But the names are heavy. They press into me until I can't tell where I end and the list begins."

Aurelian turned fully toward her. "Why tell me now?"

"Because I'm afraid," she said, simple and unhidden. "Afraid one day I'll be called to mend something I can't. And I'll stand there with my hands empty, and people will look at me and see only the promise I failed to keep." Her eyes met his. "If that happens, I don't want you to think I chose the promise over them. I want you to know I tried."

He covered her hand with his—practical, intimate, steady. "You have tried," he said. "You try every day. That is not nothing."

She let the warmth anchor her. "If I falter," she whispered, "wake me. Remind me that tending isn't only fixing. Sometimes it's staying."

Aurelian's jaw softened. "And if I falter," he said, "tell me you'll stand with me anyway."

They let the pact settle between them—not a cure, not a vow of perfection, but something human and binding. The fear didn't vanish. It simply moved—from private weight to shared ground.

When they rose to rejoin the others, their steps were steadier—not because the road had changed, but because they had given each other something to hold.

***

Moral Fork – Echoes at the Threshold

They came upon the ruined ford at dusk, where the river narrowed and the stones showed like teeth. The place smelled of wet iron and old promises. Reeds leaned away from the bank as if listening. A low wind moved through the marsh, carrying a sound that might have been a bird—or might have been the land clearing its throat.

At the water's edge, two truths waited.

The scene carried weight immediately — not the thinness of illusion, but the pressure of consequence. The Dark Land had learned how to shape more than memory now. What stood before them was not a replay, but a situation pressed into being complete and demanding.

A broken bridge sagged half submerged, its center collapsed into a dark, yawning gap. Beyond it, a small cluster of villagers huddled on the far bank, faces pale in the failing light. Their boat lay overturned, ribs exposed like a broken hand.

"They're trapped," Aurelian said. The words were simple. The river answered with a current that had teeth.

Solana stepped forward, palms open. "We can ferry them across. I can steady the weak ones. We'll make a line and pull them through."

Zophira's gaze stayed on the far bank—on the faces watching them with a mixture of hope and dread. "The ford is unstable," she said. "The current shifts. If we cross with the whole group, the stones could give. People could be swept."

Seraphiel folded his wings and looked at each of them in turn. "There is another way," he said quietly. "A narrow path through the marsh to the east. It will take longer. It will expose them to the cold night. Some will not make it without shelter."

Two doors. Neither safe. Both costly.

Aurelian's hand went to his sword as if the metal could anchor the decision. "We cannot leave them to the river. If there is a chance to get them across now, we take it."

Solana's voice trembled only slightly. "If the stones give, we will lose more than we save. I have seen currents take more than bodies—they take hope. We must not gamble with lives for the sake of speed."

Zophira drew a small circle in the mud with her stick and watched the water fill it. "What does the land ask?" she murmured. "Not what we want—but what this place can bear."

Seraphiel stepped into the shallows and let the water lap at his boots. The current tugged, testing, but did not take him. "There is no right answer," he said. "Only the answer we are willing to carry."

A voice called from the far bank—thin with cold. "Please. We have children."

The plea landed like a bell.

Aurelian's shoulders tightened. "We make a rope line. I'll go first. If the stones hold, we bring them across in pairs."

"And if they don't?" Solana asked. "Who pulls the ones who fall? Who tends the ones who drown?"

They stood with the ledger open between them: immediate rescue versus sustained care; certainty versus attrition; heroism versus endurance. Each choice carried a moral tax.

They chose together.

Not perfectly. Not safely. But with eyes open.

They moved like a single organism: Aurelian's boots found purchase; the stones groaned but held. He signaled, and the first pair — a mother and her boy — stepped into the line. The rope bit into hands, the current tugged, and for a breath the world narrowed to the sound of water and the rhythm of pulling. They made it across. Then another pair. Then the old man, who slipped and was caught by two strong arms before the river could claim him.

But the river is a teacher of humility. Midway through the crossing, a stone shifted with a sound like a small breaking. A child's scream cut the air as water took a foot and then a leg. Solana dove, hands working with the practiced speed of someone who had learned to move in the space between life and loss. They pulled the child free, coughing and shivering, but alive.

When the last villager reached the far bank, they were wet and trembling and grateful in a way that made the quartet's chests ache. They had chosen, and the choice had cost them — a near loss, a scraped knee, a night of fevered sleep for one small body. But they had also saved a cluster of lives that might otherwise have been lost to slow attrition.

That night, as they tended the villagers by the fire, each of them carried the weight of the decision. They had acted with courage and with caution, and both had left their marks. The moral ledger did not close; it simply shifted. They had learned that sometimes the only honest choice is the one you are willing to bear the consequences of, together.

They returned to the clearing with the river's breath on their backs. The villagers slept in a cluster of blankets, the small bodies rising and falling like a single, fragile tide.

Sleep took them hard and without ceremony.

When Aurelian woke, the fire had burned down to ash. The river still moved beside them — unchanged, unsoftened. The clearing was empty.

No blankets. No bodies. No breath rising and falling.

The realization settled slowly, like cold in the bones. The crossing had been real to them — the choice, the cost, the weight of it — but nothing remained. The land had set the moment and then withdrawn, leaving them with what their decision had made of them.

They were still in the Dark Land.

Aurelian sat again on his jagged rock, hands folded, the tightness in his chest now threaded with something else — a tired relief and a new, quieter doubt.

Aurelian's doubt pressed at him like a tide. Is my strength actually useful anymore? The question had been a quiet whisper in his mind for days, but now it roared like a storm. He had always seen himself as the one who carried others, the one who stood firm when the ground gave way. But the battles they'd faced had chipped away at that certainty, exposing cracks he hadn't known were there. Images flashed through his mind — moments when he'd faltered, when his courage hadn't been enough. The Wrathbearer's words echoed: You carry it for others; How long can this keep working? He clenched his fists; nails digging into his palms, and the doubt sat heavy in his chest.

Zophira crouched near the edge of the river, her fingers tracing slow, deliberate patterns in the cracked dirt. The water's surface shimmered faintly, but her reflection refused to settle — fractured, bending, slipping out of shape each time she tried to meet her own eyes. She looked away before it could distort again.

Her thoughts spiraled, not in panic, but in a quiet, relentless loop. What if the land cannot be read? The question pressed at her temples like a dull ache.

She had seen the crossing clearly. She had measured the current, the stones, the risk. Her clarity had held — and yet the land had not shifted. Nothing had resolved. Nothing had revealed itself. The truth she trusted had not anchored anything.

Perplexia's laughter drifted through her memory, thin and sharp. What if nothing here wants to be known?

Zophira's hand tightened around a small stone until it slipped from her grip and fell into the mud. She watched the water creep into the imprint it left behind, filling it without shape or intention.

If the world refuses to be read, she thought, what does that make a Seer?

The river murmured on, indifferent. And for the first time, her clarity felt like a lantern held up to fog — light intact, but unable to reveal the path ahead.

Solana leaned against a gnarled tree; the vial of water cradled in her hands glowing faintly — its light a fragile pulse in the dim. Am I erasing myself? The question lingered, sharp and unrelenting.

She had always been the healer, the one who carried warmth into cold places, who steadied others when their strength faltered. But the shadows had revealed a truth she had never dared to name: every time she poured herself into another life, something of her own slipped away unnoticed.

The Apathetic Void's whisper clung to her like damp air. You give and give… but what remains of you, Solana?

Her grip tightened around the vial. She thought of the faces she had healed, the trembling hands she had held, the small bodies she had pulled back from the edge — and the exhaustion that followed each act like a quiet tide.

What if there is nothing left of me to restore? The vial's glow flickered, as if answering a question, she wasn't ready to face.

Seraphiel stood at the edge of the clearing, wings folded tight against his back. Their faint glow had dimmed to a thin, wavering shimmer — not extinguished, but uncertain, like a lantern held too far from its own flame.

Why am I still shining? The question pulsed through him, steady and relentless.

He had always been the guide, the one who sensed the path when others could not, who carried light into places that had forgotten what light was. But here, in the Dark Land, his glow felt fragile — not because it was fading, but because it no longer seemed to change anything.

The Void's voice lingered in the back of his mind, cold and patient. What difference does it make? All light fades.

Seraphiel exhaled slowly, watching the breath leave him like a thin ribbon of mist. He thought of the crossing — how he had read the currents, how he had found the safer path, how he had steadied the others with instinct alone. His guidance had been true. His light had held.

And yet the land had not softened. The darkness had not shifted. Nothing had answered back.

His wings twitched, the glow along their edges flickering as though caught in a wind he could not feel.

If light does not change the darkness, he wondered, then what is the purpose of shining at all?

The question did not break him. It simply hollowed a quiet space inside him — a space where meaning used to rest.

The River of Process flowed on, its surface rippling faintly as if mirroring their unease. The quartet remained silent, each lost in their own thoughts, their own doubts. The weight of the Dark Land pressed heavily on them, its shadows reaching into the cracks they had tried to keep hidden. For now, there were no answers, no clarity or resolve. Only the silence of the land around them and the quiet hum of the river as it carried them forward, whether they were ready or not.

***

Zophira at the Pool

The others slept in uneasy knots of blankets, their breaths shallow in the morning gloom. Zophira moved away from the clearing, drawn by a pull she could not name. The river's murmur guided her east, where the trees thinned and the ground dipped into a quiet hollow.

A pool waited there — still, dark, perfectly round, as if the land had carved a single held breath into the earth.

Zophira knelt at its edge.

The surface was glass-smooth, untouched by wind or current. It should have shown her reflection clearly. It should have anchored her. Instead, the moment she leaned over it, the water shivered — not from movement, but from refusal.

Her reflection blurred at the edges, then fractured into thin, wavering lines. Eyes she recognized. Eyes she didn't. A face that was hers, and not hers, shifting in ways she could not track.

She exhaled slowly, steadying her breath.

"Show me," she whispered — not a command, not a plea. A request for truth.

The pool did not answer.

The surface rippled once, as if something beneath it had turned away. Her reflection broke into a scatter of shapes, none of them holding long enough to read.

Zophira's fingers curled into the dirt.

If the land cannot be known… then what am I meant to see?

She dipped her hand into the water. It was cold — not biting, not cruel, simply indifferent. The ripples spread outward, distorting the fragments of her face until they dissolved entirely.

For a moment, she felt the old certainty rise in her — the instinct to name, to interpret, to cut through the haze. But the pool offered nothing to cut through. No illusion. No deception. Just a truth she could not grasp.

A truth that refused to take shape.

Zophira withdrew her hand and sat back on her heels. The water stilled again, returning to its perfect, unreadable calm.

Behind her, the Dark Land stretched in every direction, silent and watching.

If clarity cannot find purchase here, she thought, then what guides me?

The question settled in her chest like a stone — not heavy, but undeniable.

She rose, brushing dirt from her palms. The pool remained unchanged, a dark eye set on the earth, reflecting nothing she could use.

Zophira turned away from it and walked back toward the clearing, her steps measured, her breath steady. The land had not given her an answer.

But it had shown her the shape of the question she would have to carry.

***

Travel Conversation: River Crossing

They moved at first light, the river at their shoulder and the road a ribbon of damp earth. The crossing that morning was slow — not the urgent scramble of the ford but the careful, measured pace of people who had learned to keep one another whole. The mist lifted in thin curtains, and the world smelled of wet stone and new green. Aurelian walked near the front, boots steady, but his steps were quieter than usual. At a bend in the river he paused and turned, as if the land itself had asked him to look back. Solana fell into step beside him, carrying a small bundle of herbs and a wrapped loaf. You always check the banks twice," she said, not a question but an observation that had the shape of a kindness. He shrugged. "Old habit. The ground tells you things if you listen."

She watched him for a long moment. "What do you hear now?"

He considered the river, the way it moved around a half-submerged stone. "That we're tired," he said finally. "That we keep moving because stopping feels like admitting we can't do it."

Solana's hand brushed his sleeve. "You don't have to carry the stopping alone."

He let out a breath that might have been a laugh. "I know. I just… I forget sometimes that asking for help is not the same as failing."

They walked on, and the conversation folded into the rhythm of their steps. Further back, Zophira and Seraphiel walked side by side, their voices low enough that the river kept most of their words.

Zophira kicked at a pebble and watched it tumble. "When I was a child," she said, "my mother would make me chart the tides for hours. She said the sea would teach me patience."

Seraphiel smiled. "And did it?"

"It taught me to trust patterns," she said. "But it also taught me to believe the map more than the people who lived by it. I'm trying to unlearn that."

Seraphiel's hand found hers for a moment. "Maps are useful," he said. "But they are not the only language. People speak in breath and in small gestures. I learned that when I had to wake someone who would not answer to words."

Zophira's laugh was soft. "You wake people with questions?"

"With a question that asks them to notice their breath," Seraphiel said. "It's harder to hide from a question about breathing."

They fell quiet, and the river filled the space. The crossing itself was uneventful — a narrow ford, stones slick with moss, hands linked where the current tugged. On the far bank they paused to rest, and a child from a passing village offered them a handful of wildflowers with the solemnity of a small ambassador.

Aurelian accepted the flowers and tucked them into his pack. "I used to think courage was a thing you could measure," he said later, when the group had spread out on a sun warmed rock. "But now I think it's the willingness to keep showing up when you're afraid."

Solana nodded. "And the willingness to be seen when you're not whole."

Zophira traced a line in the dirt with her stick. "We are learning to carry each other's edges," she said. "Not to smooth them out, but to hold them so they don't cut us."

Seraphiel looked at each of them in turn. "That is the work," he said. "Not to erase the dark, but to make room for it without letting it take the whole table."

Aurelian's gaze drifted to the river, then back to his companions. "Then we keep walking," he said. "Together."

They rose and shouldered their packs, the river's song at their backs. The crossing had not solved anything, but it had shifted something small and necessary: a confession, a habit named, a hand offered and taken. The road ahead remained uncertain, but for the moment their steps matched, and that was enough.

They left the clearing with the river at their shoulder, the moral ledger heavy but shared. The night had taught them that choices in the Dark Land carried consequences that did not end with the act; they lingered, shaped the small hours, and altered how each of them would answer the next call. They walked on together, not because the path was clear, but because they had chosen to carry the weight as one.

Chapter 12: SINKING SHADOWS

The landscape of the Dark Land shifted into something more sinister. The once fractured terrain smoothed into a deceptive calm, its surface slick with an unnatural sheen, reflecting distorted fragments of the quartet as they moved. The ground beneath them was damp, almost spongy, giving the illusion of stability while pulling subtly at their feet with each step.

The River of Process had narrowed alongside them, its waters now a deep, inky black that carried an unsettling shimmer, as if it were swallowing light rather than reflecting it. A faint, rhythmic thrumming resonated from it, like a heartbeat — slow, deliberate, and ominous. It wasn't just the land that felt alive, but the river itself, watching and waiting.

"This place is wrong," Zophira murmured, her voice cutting through the uneasy quiet. "It's too still, like it's holding its breath before something happens."

The terrain sloped downward, the quartet descending into what appeared to be a basin carved by time and despair. Jagged rocks jutted out at unnatural angles, their surfaces glistening with a dark, tar-like substance. What little light Seraphiel's wings emitted was swallowed whole by the looming shadows, giving the impression they were walking deeper into a chasm without end.

Then came the sound — a soft squelching beneath their feet. The ground shifted, no longer spongy but wet and sticky. Aurelian paused, lifting one boot to reveal the dark muck clinging to it, viscous and clinging. The more they moved, the more the ground seemed to grab hold, as though it had awakened.

"It's pulling us," Seraphiel said, his wings stretching instinctively. "The land isn't just still — it's waiting."

The quartet tried to retreat, but the muck held firm. The ground beneath them rippled, the surface splitting into tendrils that rose up, twisting and curling as they encircled the group. They fought to move, but each motion dragged them further down.

"It's alive!" Solana cried, gripping her vial tightly as the shadows began

to engulf them. From the blackened mire came shapes, uncoiling like smoke given form. Their edges were sharp yet indistinct, constantly shifting and blurring. Voices followed — layered, hollow, and familiar.

"Did you think we were gone?"

The tendrils tightened around their waists as the shadows solidified into figures. First came Fearmonger, its form distorted and jagged, the malice in its presence sharp enough to cut. Its laughter was low, crawling into their minds. "You cannot outrun fear. It grows with you."

Beside it, Wrathbearer emerged, its flames reduced to glowing embers, yet no less menacing. "You smothered your anger, but it still burns within, waiting for a chance to consume you."

Then came the others: the Shadow Keeper, its hollow gaze fixed on them; the Apathetic Void, an imposing specter of indifference; and finally, Perplexia, swirling around the group, its erratic movements disorienting. Together, the shadows closed in, their combined presence suffocating and relentless.

"Did you think one victory would banish us?" Fearmonger asked, its voice sharp and mocking. "We are not obstacles to be overcome. We are part of you."

The ground beneath them seemed to sink further, dragging them down inch by inch. The shadows' voices grew louder, overlapping into a cacophony of taunts and accusations.

"You are weak!" Wrathbearer snarled. "Your rage will destroy you!"
"You are lost," Perplexia whispered, its voice slithering through their thoughts. "And you will never find your way."

"You are nothing," the Void intoned, its monotone final and absolute.

The quartet struggled, their movements sluggish as though the very air had thickened. Their gifts flickered faintly, the light from Seraphiel's wings paling against the encroaching darkness. The River of Process churned violently beside them, its waters rising as if responding to the chaos.

Aurelian's muscles strained as he tried to free himself, but the shadows' words burrowed into his mind. What if they're right? What if my strength has always been a mask for my weakness?

The doubt did not land like a blow. It landed like recognition — the quiet, sickening kind that comes when someone names the thing you have spent your entire life outrunning. His arms, thick with the memory of every burden lifted, trembled not from effort but from the sudden question of whether any of it had mattered. The mire climbed higher, and he let it, because for one terrible moment the sinking felt like honesty.

Zophira's hands trembled, her thoughts swirling like a storm. I've always relied on clarity, but what if I've been wrong? What if I've misled them all?

The storm was not new. She had felt it before — in quiet moments when a pattern dissolved under closer examination, when an answer she had been certain of revealed itself as assumption wearing certainty's clothes. But those moments had been private, containable. Here, with the mire pulling at her legs and the shadows pressing close, the storm broke through every wall she had built to contain it. Her mind, her one reliable instrument, played every wrong note it had ever struck at once. The cacophony was unbearable not because it was loud but because it was accurate.

Solana clutched the vial tightly, her fingers white-knuckled. I've given everything I have, but it's never enough. What if I can't heal this time?

The vial pulsed faintly against her palm, and for the first time the warmth felt like accusation rather than comfort. She had poured so much of herself into others that the vessel had become more real than the woman holding it. The mire reached her hips now, and some part of her — the part she never let anyone see — wondered if sinking might be simpler than the endless work of rising for someone else. The thought horrified her.

And the horror itself was a kind of proof: she still cared. But caring while drowning felt less like a gift and more like a sentence she had written for herself in ink she could not wash away.

Seraphiel's wings faltered, their glow dimming. I've carried the light, but what if it was never enough to guide us? What if I've already failed them?

The dimming did not feel like loss. That was the worst part. It felt like permission — the kind no one gives you but the dark. His wings had been his proof of worth for so long that their fading registered not as failure but as a question he had refused to ask: what if the light had never been for them at all? What if it had always been for him to make himself necessary, to ensure that no one could walk away from someone who lit their path? The mire reached his waist, and in its cold grip he felt the shape of a truth he had carried since before the Dark Land: the terror was never the darkness. The terror was discovering he had built his entire self around the fear of it.

The shadows surged, their forms tightening around the group. The River of Process swelled, its waters breaking free of their banks to lap at their feet. The rhythmic thrum from the river grew louder, deeper, as though the land itself was echoing their despair.

The quartet sank further into the muck, their struggles weakening. The shadows' voices grew louder, drowning out the river, drowning out everything but their doubts and fears.

The chapter closes with the group trapped, the shadows pressing closer, their unity fractured under the weight of their own inner turmoil. For now, there is no escape, no resolution — only the relentless pull of the Dark Land and the echoes of their own doubts.

Chapter 13: CRACKS IN THE LIGHT

The village woke to a sky that felt wrong, not dark, not stormy, but thin, as if someone had stretched a pale cloth over the sun. The River of Process, which usually moved with a steady, sure voice, now whispered in fits and starts; its surface caught light in odd, jittering flashes. People noticed it first in the small, practical ways they always noticed things: a net that would not hold a knot, a wheel that shuddered when it turned, a loaf that browned unevenly in the oven.

At the edge of the fields, Doran walked the rows with his hands on his hips, testing the soil. The earth crumbled differently beneath his fingers, and was dry where it should hold moisture, clinging where it should give. He tapped a seed into the furrow and watched it sit on the surface as if the ground had forgotten how to take it. He did not shout or point fingers; he called the miller and the elder who kept the planting lists. Together they measured, marked, and decided: which beds to leave fallow, which to water by hand, and who would trade seed for labor. The work was practical and immediate; it did not fix the land, but it kept the village fed for another season.

Animals moved with a new, restless intelligence. The herd by the river paced in tighter circles, heads low, eyes bright and unblinking. Dogs that had always slept through storms woke and paced the lanes, noses to the air. The blacksmith's mare refused the harness she had worn for years; she stamped and turned away from the cart as if the road itself had become a thing to avoid. Thaddeus did not curse the animal. He sat on the cart's edge and ran his hands along the mare's flank until her breathing slowed. Then he tightened a strap, checked a wheel, and walked the path himself to see what the mare had seen: a low, distant shimmer in the fields, like heat without warmth.

Birds were the first to show the change in a way that could not be explained away. The Starlings — usually a playful, harmless presence at dusk — began to gather in odd clusters, landing on roofs and wires with a nervous, clipped precision. At first people mentioned it in passing: an oddness to the flock, a hush when they passed. Then one morning a flock dove low over the market, not in the carefree swoop of play but with sharp, purposeful strikes. A fisherman's crate toppled; fish skittered across the cobbles. Villagers screamed. Traders tried to move with the practiced motions of people who had to protect their goods;: tarps were thrown, animals herded, nets checked. Selene steadied the fisherman's hands and tied the crate down herself. The birds' aggression was a spectacle; it was a noted crisis that would ripple through the week's bread and the next month's accounts.

The River itself began to behave like it had a mind of its own. In some stretches it slowed to a glassy, reflective stillness that held the sky like a secret; in others it surged with a sudden, cold current that tugged at ropes and overturned small boats. The ferryman's rope line at the narrow ford frayed in one place and snapped in another; a small skiff drifted free and had to be hauled back by three men. The crossing that had been routine now required a watch and a rope. The elders posted names and times on the pavilion door, of those assigned to check the river crossings in the morning and who would carry the sick and old across., who would keep the lamps lit along the bank.

At the market, the miller closed his ledger and ran his thumb along the inked lines as if the numbers might rearrange themselves into sense. He did not shout. He called for extra hands to help sift grain and for a rotation of watch at the ford. The ledger was not a talisman; it was a tool. People answered with the small, steady work that keeps a place from unraveling: mending nets, patching roofs, checking the well's depth. Where there had been arguments before, there were now lists and schedules and the quiet exchange of labor for food.

The elders met in the pavilion, but their meeting was not a string of speeches. They opened maps and old ledgers, traced the river's bends with a finger, and assigned tasks. Elder Myrial walked the market afterward, not to lecture but to hand a woven patch to a woman whose stall had been damaged and to show a young man how to tie a proper watch rope. Elder Tovrik took the oar from a trembling villager and taught him the angle to hold it against the current. The work of leadership here was not pronouncement; it was the steadying of hands and the passing on of small, useful skills.

At night the sounds changed. The usual chorus of frogs and distant laughter was punctuated by sharp, unfamiliar cries: a flock of birds that rose and fell like a living wave, a pack of goats that scattered and then reassembled in a different field, a dog that howled and then fell silent. People slept in shifts, not out of panic but because the river's new moods demanded someone awake to notice the first change. Those who watched did not pray for answers; they checked the ropes, stoked the coals, and kept the lamps lit.

A few incidents were harder to explain. A fishing boat that had left at dawn returned at dusk with its nets full of pale weeds that smelled faintly of salt though the sea was miles away. A flock of geese that had nested by the eastern marsh took flight in a single, panicked burst and did not return. A woman who tended the village's oldest apple tree found the bark split in a clean, vertical line as if some cold blade had passed through it. Each event was small on its own, but together they formed a pattern the village could not ignore.

People began to mark the land in practical ways. Stones were set at the ford to show the safest stepping points. A rope line was strung across the narrowest crossing for those who could not swim. The blacksmith fashioned extra hooks for nets and reinforced the carts' axles. Maelis wove a new pattern into her cloth — a braid of river knots meant to remind hands how to hold. These were not charms against fate; they were tools and reminders, the kind of work that made a community resilient.

Rumors moved through the lanes, but they were not the loud, blaming rumors of old. They were the quiet exchanges of people trying to make sense: "The river took the old willow last night." "My mare wouldn't cross the east field." "The starlings have been circling the mill." Each sentence ended with a plan: who would check the willow, who would lead the mare, who would stand watch at the mill. The village's response was practical because it had to be fear without action would only hollow them out.

By the time the quartet returned to the clearing, the change in the land was visible in the small, adult ways that mattered most. The square bore the marks of people who had chosen to act patched roofs, a new rope coiled by the ford, a ledger with extra columns for watch rotations. The elders did not ask for miracles. They asked for hands. The quartet did not arrive to be hailed as saviors; they arrived to join the work.

The land had cracked, but it had not broken. The cracks showed where attention was needed. The animals and elements were not enemies to be driven off; they were signals. The village's task was not to banish the signs but to learn how to live with them: to tend the river's moods, to mend what the weather and the wild had frayed, and to keep the ordinary, steady work of life going while they learned what the land was asking.

Night fell with a cautious hush. Lamps were lit along the riverbank, not as a show but as a practical measure: light for those who watched, warmth for those who could not sleep, a steady line for boats that might need to find their way. The village did not sleep easily, but it did not panic. It moved with the deliberate, adult rhythm of people who had learned that survival was a series of small, shared acts — and that sometimes the most important thing was simply to keep showing up.

Chapter 14: FRACTURED FOUNDATIONS

The Council Pavilion, once a symbol of harmony and guidance, now felt stifling to the Elders gathered within its walls. The table at its center, polished smooth by years of steady hands and deliberation, seemed colder now, a reflection of their faltering unity. Outside, the muffled hum of the village carried a tense, unsettled energy, like a fire smoldering just beneath the surface.

Elder Myrial sat at the head of the table, her fingers tracing the grooves of an old carving etched into its edge. It was a symbol of balance, a reminder of their purpose as guides and protectors of the Land of Soul. But today, it felt more like a relic of a time that was slipping away.

"We've kept order before," Myrial said, her voice steady but low. "Through floods, through droughts, through hardship. But this… this feels different."

"This isn't a drought or a flood," Elder Tovrik replied sharply, his hands flat on the table. "This is the land itself turning against us. The River of Process is slowing. The creatures are changing. "The people"; He hesitated, lowering his gaze. "The people are losing faith in themselves, in us; in everything!"

"And perhaps they should," Elder Lirien said softly, her voice carrying an edge of bitterness. She looked out through the pavilion's open archway, her expression distant. "We've relied so long on the river's flow, on the land's harmony, that we forgot how fragile it all is. How fragile we are."

Her words hung in the air, heavy with unspoken fears. Myrial frowned, her heart aching at the cracks forming within their council. If we falter, what hope does the village have?

In the village square, a group of children huddled together near the old well, their voices hushed. The events of the day — the starlings, the growing tension — had left them uneasy, their usual games replaced by quiet whispers and furtive glances.

"Do you think the shadows are real?" Mira asked, clutching her sketchbook tightly to her chest. She had drawn the starlings from memory, their jagged forms etched in dark charcoal. The image made her shiver. "I don't know," Lina replied, her voice uncharacteristically subdued. "But something's wrong with the land. You can feel it. Everything feels… mean."

"What if the shadows are coming for us?" Tavin whispered, his wide eyes darting to the forest's edge. "What if they're already here?"

Jorin, standing slightly apart from the group, frowned. "They're not coming for us," he said firmly. "The quartet will stop them. That's what everyone says."

"But what if they don't?" Mira asked, her voice trembling. "What if they can't?"

The children fell silent, their imaginations filling the gaps left by their elders' reassurances. The forest, once a place of wonder and adventure, now seemed dark and foreboding. Every rustle of the leaves, every shift of the shadows, felt like a threat waiting to emerge.

Back in the pavilion, the Elders continued their strained discussion. Myrial stood, her chair scraping against the floor as she turned to face the room. "We've always drawn strength from the truths of our history," she said, her voice firm. "The river flows. The light prevails. The balance is maintained. But perhaps we've misunderstood the balance."

Tovrik frowned. "What are you suggesting?"

"Balance isn't the lack of hardship," Myrial said. "It's knowing how to endure, and how to change your steps when the ground shifts, and we, as Elders, must do the same."

Lirien sighed, shaking her head. "Endure? Adapt? The people are looking to us for answers, Myrial, not more riddles. How can we guide them when we don't even understand what's happening?"

Myrial's gaze softened, and she placed a hand on the table. "By acknowledging our own fear. By admitting that we don't have all the answers — but that we are willing to search for them."

The council fell silent, each elder retreating into their thoughts. Myrial's words carried weight, but they also exposed the truth they had been avoiding, that their own doubts and fears mirrored those of the villagers. The shadows weren't just in the Dark Land — they were here, creeping into the hearts of all who lived in the Land of Soul.

Near the edge of the village, the children had wandered closer to the forest, their curiosity outweighing their fear. The trees stood like sentinels, their dark branches twisting into unnatural shapes. Mira knelt beside a patch of earth, her fingers brushing against something shiny.

"It's a feather," she whispered, holding it up for the others to see. It shimmered faintly, a remnant of the starlings they had encountered. But as she turned it in her hands, the shimmer faded, replaced by a dull, ashen gray.

"Put it down," Jorin said, his voice sharp. "It's not safe."

Mira hesitated but obeyed, dropping the feather as if it had burned her. The group huddled together, their unease growing as the forest seemed to shift around them.

Then came the sound — a low, guttural growl that froze them in place. From the shadows emerged a creature unlike anything they had seen before. Its form was twisted, its fur matted and blackened, its eyes glowing faintly with an unnatural light.

The children screamed, scrambling back toward the village as the creature advanced, its movements jerky and aggressive. The once-gentle beasts of the forest had become something else — something darker.

They burst into the square, their cries drawing the attention of the villagers. Selene rushed forward, gathering Mira and Lina into her arms. "What happened?" she asked, her voice frantic.

"There was a creature," Jorin gasped, his face pale. "It wasn't like the others. It… it wanted to hurt us."

The villagers murmured anxiously, their fear spreading like wildfire. Myrial emerged from the pavilion, her expression grave as she took in the children's panic.

"The shadows," someone whispered. "They're spreading."

Myrial's heart sank as the murmurs grew louder, the villagers' unease threatening to spiral into chaos. She stepped forward, her voice firm. "We will protect this village. But we must stay united. Fear will not save us — only trust and courage will."

Her words calmed the crowd, if only slightly. But as the villagers dispersed, Myrial felt the weight of their doubts pressing against her. She looked toward the forest, its darkened edge seeming to pulse with life.

Whatever is happening in the Dark Land, it is no longer confined there, she thought. And time is running out.

Chapter 15: BOUND BY SHADOWS

The ground gave way beneath their feet.

At first it was subtle — a trembling, a shiver in the soil — then the earth lurched violently, releasing a thick, blackened mire that clung to their boots like something alive. The River of Process churned beside them, no longer whispering but groaning as if in pain.

Aurelian was the first to sense the shift. "Move back," he warned —

but too late.

The mud rose with a sickening slurp, wrapping around their ankles, pulling hard. The quartet staggered, struggling to free themselves, but the land swallowed them faster with every movement.

"It's pulling us under!" Solana cried, the glow of her vial flickering desperately.

The mire spread up their legs, thickening, tightening, as if it recognized each of them personally — and meant to consume them whole.

The cold was not weather-cold. It was the temperature of being known — the chill that comes when something sees past every defense and settles against the skin you keep hidden. Aurelian felt it climb his thighs like iron bands tightening, each inch a memory of every time he had stood firm when his body screamed to run. Zophira felt it as pressure against her temples, the mire somehow reaching for her thoughts, pressing against the architecture of her mind like water testing a dam. Solana felt warmth leaving her body in layers — first her hands, then her arms, then the center of her chest where she kept the heat she gave to others. Seraphiel felt his wings stiffen and drag downward, the mire coating the feathers with a weight that was not mud but accumulated silence — every truth he had swallowed to keep shining.

Then the shadows came. Not one.

Not two. All of them.

Fearmonger slithered out of the dark first, its form jagged with delight.

"You thought fear was finished with you?" it hissed. "Fear never ends.

Fear evolves."

Behind it, Wrathbearer rose like molten rage, embers swirling through the air.

"You swallowed your fire," it growled. "Now feel the burn of everything you denied."

The Shadow Keeper emerged next — its presence colder than before, heavier, as though the weight of every memory had doubled.

"You carry lessons," it whispered, "but refuse to carry truth. Your past is not finished with you."

The Apathetic Void drifted silently, its presence draining the air of all warmth.

"There is no meaning," it murmured. "Not here. Not anywhere."

Then Perplexia twirled into existence, shifting shape with nauseating speed.

"You can't choose!" it taunted. "You'll only choose wrong! You always have!"

The shadows circled, merging, intensifying. The air grew thick — too thick to breathe.

Aurelian pulled against the mire with all his strength, but it held him fast, dragging him downward inch by merciless inch.

Fearmonger leaned close, whispering into the cracks of his resolve.

"You can't protect anyone," it said. "Not now. Not ever. You didn't save them then. You won't save them now."

Aurelian's muscles trembled. "No—no, I—"

But the shadow's words hit the old wounds he buried deepest, and his shield flickered.

Zophira fought to steady her mind, but Perplexia spiraled around her, filling her thoughts with a storm of uncertainty.

"You see nothing clearly," it sang. "You only think you do. Every insight? A mistake. Every decision? A misstep."

Her breath fractured. Her clarity blurred.

What if it's right?

What if I have been wrong all along?

Solana tried to lift her vial, but the mire dragged her arm down, pinning her wrist in cold darkness.

"You've healed no one," the Apathetic Void whispered. "They recovered on their own. Your efforts were illusions. Your gift? A lie you told yourself to feel needed."

Her heart seized.

Her hands trembled so hard the vial nearly slipped from her grasp. Seraphiel stood frozen, his wings darkened at the tips. The Shadow

Keeper moved behind him, its voice low and merciless.

"Your light wasn't taken," it said. "You abandoned it. You allowed it to

dim. Because you are afraid of what you are in the dark."

Seraphiel felt something inside him fracture — a soundless, private breaking.

The Wrathbearer roared, and flames ignited around them. Heat seared the air, making their skin prickle. "You denied your anger," it bellowed. "Now it devours you from within."

The quartet strained, gasped, fought — but the shadows pressed harder, layering their assault until each whisper felt like a strike.

Fear. Rage. Guilt.

Numbness. Confusion. Emptiness. All at once.

It became impossible to tell which feeling belonged to whom — or if any of the feelings still belonged to them at all.

Aurelian's courage cracked. Zophira's clarity shattered. Solana's compassion waned.

Seraphiel's light dimmed to the faintest ember.

The mire pulled them lower. Up to their knees.

Up to their waists.

The land felt alive — hungry — dragging them into a grave of their own shadows.

Fearmonger whispered, "You cannot outrun fear…" Wrathbearer added,

"You cannot smother fire…"

The Shadow Keeper folded in closer,

"You cannot escape the past…"

The Void whispered,

"You cannot create meaning…"

Perplexia trilled,

"You cannot know the way…"

Their voices merged into a single, crushing truth:

"You cannot win."

Solana gasped as the mire reached her chest.

"Aurelian—Seraphiel—Zophira—I can't—"

Aurelian tried to reach her, but his arms were pinned against the rising muck.

"I can't move!"

Zophira's voice shook violently.

"I can't see — I can't think — I can't—"

Seraphiel struggled for breath, his wings nearly swallowed.

"My light… I can't find my light…"

For the first time since entering the Dark Land, the quartet broke. Cracked open.

Splintered by the weight of every shadow they had avoided, denied, outrun, or tried to carry alone.

The shadows drew nearer, closing in until the quartet could feel their cold breath, their heat, their static, their emptiness — all pressing against their skin.

Fearmonger whispered,

"Let go."

Wrathbearer's voice thundered,

"Fall!"

The Void murmured,

"Sink."

Perplexia chanted,

"Lose yourself."

The mire reached their shoulders. Their chins.

Their mouths.

Just before the darkness consumed them — just before the world fell silent —

The River of Process surged violently, roaring like a creature awakened. The shadows recoiled — just an inch — as the water rose in a sudden,

furious whirl, its surface shimmering with something raw and ancient.

But the quartet could not rise. They could not breathe.

They could not see.

They could only feel themselves slipping under the weight of fear, weight of guilt, weight of unspoken truth.

Bound. Breaking. Sinking.

The quartet was pulled into the darkness. The land held its' breath.

Chapter 16: SURRENDER TO THE TRUTH

Darkness swallowed them whole.

Not the simple absence of light, but the suffocating kind — heavy, intimate, the kind that presses against the bones and whispers truths you've spent a lifetime avoiding.

The mire dragged them under completely, sealing their limbs, their lungs, their voices. For a moment, there was no sense of body at all — only pressure, heaviness, and the echo of every shadow they had ever carried.

Fearmonger. Wrathbearer.

The Shadow Keeper. The Void.

Perplexia.

Each voice pressed inward, merging into a single, crushing presence:

"Fall. Sink. Break."

Aurelian felt the weight first — a crushing, immovable pressure that pinned him down until he could no longer distinguish the mire from the shame in his own chest.

His strength was gone. His shield was gone. His role was gone.

All he could hear was a whisper that sounded like himself:

What am I if I can't protect anyone?

What am I without my strength?

Zophira felt her mind fracturing under the swirl of confusion. Her insight — once sharp — now felt like shards of glass cutting inward.

Her inner voice trembled:

What if I never saw clearly? What if I led us into ruin?

Solana felt the ache of every life she tried to hold together. The mire pressed against her heart, squeezing until she felt hollow, scraped out.

Her inner voice cracked:

Have I healed others because I'm empty inside? What if I give because I don't know how to be?

Seraphiel felt his wings crushed by the weight of unseen truth. His light

— so bright for others — had dimmed into the faintest flicker.

His inner voice dimmed:

What if my light was never real?

What if I've always been pretending?

For a long, unmeasured moment, there was nothing left. No fight. No hope. No names. Just the weight of every truth they had spent their lives outrunning, pressing them into the dark like hands pressing a body into earth. Aurelian's fingers uncurled — not by choice, but because the muscles had finally given out. Zophira's mind, for the first time in her life, went completely silent. Solana felt her heartbeat slow to something barely there, a candle guttering in a sealed room. Seraphiel's wings folded inward, pressed flat against his back, and he felt the darkness close over them like water over a stone. This was the edge. Not of death — but of the self they had always known.

The shadows swirled closer, sensing the rupture. But then—

A pulse. Soft.

Steady. Ancient.

The River of Process.

Even submerged in the choking dark, they could still feel it — beating like a second heart, calling them home.

It was not a rescue. It was a reminder.

The river whispered — not with sound, but with essence: Stop fighting.

Feel.

The words landed not in their ears but in their chests — a vibration that loosened something ancient and clenched. It was terrifying. To stop fighting meant to stop being the thing they had always been. It meant standing in the wreckage of every role, every shield, every carefully maintained identity — and finding out what was left. The river did not rush them. It waited.

Aurelian's breath shuddered.

He stopped resisting guilt. He stopped pushing it away. He let himself feel the truth:

I am afraid.

Just saying it — inside himself — made something lessen.

His jaw unclenched. A shudder moved through his shoulders — not weakness, but the body's recognition that it had been holding a weight it was never meant to carry alone. The mire around his arms softened, just barely, like soil after the first rain.

Zophira let the confusion wash over her without trying to fix it, order it, or solve it.

I don't know everything, she admitted silently.

I never did.

The mire loosened around her ribs.

Her hands, which had been gripping at nothing, went still. The sharpness behind her eyes — the one that had always been searching, always calculating — dimmed to something quieter. Not blindness. Rest.

Solana released the lifelong tension of carrying everyone's pain but her own. Her heart whispered, fragile but honest: I hurt too.

Warmth flickered in her palms.

The words cracked open something she had sealed so long ago she had forgotten it was there. Her palms, always extended outward, turned upward. Receiving. For the first time, she did not reach for someone else's wound. She held her own.

Seraphiel let the last scrap of his forced light extinguish — not in defeat, but in surrender. And in the darkness beneath even that light, he found something quieter, smaller, but more real: I am worthy even without the glow.

His wings trembled — not with effort, but with release. The tension that had kept them bright kept them performing, drained away like water from cupped hands. And in its place, a stillness that felt more honest than any light he had ever cast.

A faint shimmer rose from the river. The shadows hissed.

Fearmonger recoiled first. Wrathbearer flickered.

The Void trembled. Perplexia spiraled erratically.

The Keeper watched in silence, waiting. Then — two new figures emerged.

Shadowess shifted into a thousand faces, each one reflecting a fragment of Aurelian, Zophira, Solana, Seraphiel.

Aurelian saw his own face hardened into granite — the version of himself that never flinched, never asked, never broke. Zophira saw herself with eyes like locked doors, brilliant and unreachable. Solana saw hands always reaching outward, palms never turning toward herself. Seraphiel saw wings spread wide, blazing, beautiful — and behind them, a figure hunched and hollow, hiding in the glare. Each reflection lingered long enough to ache.

Her voice was silken, familiar, frightening.

"Who are you," she asked, "beneath the masks you've worn?"

Her eyes glimmered with the sharpness of their most painful truths.

"And what remains," she whispered, "when the roles fall away?"

Next came Celeve, her presence soft but piercing — the voice of compassion twisted into accountability.

She touched each of them lightly, not with force but with recognition.

Her fingers carried the temperature of truth — not cold, not warm, but precise. Where she touched Aurelian's shoulder, the muscle unknotted. Where she pressed Zophira's temple, the relentless hum of analysis quieted. Where she laid her palm against Solana's sternum, the hollowness filled — not with purpose, but with permission. Where she brushed Seraphiel's folded wing, the feathers stirred as though remembering what it felt like to rest.

"You give so much," she said, "yet you have abandoned yourselves." Her gaze softened on Solana.

"Selflessness without self-love becomes self-erasure." She faced Zophira.

"Wisdom without vulnerability becomes walls."

She turned to Aurelian.

"Strength without truth becomes burden." She touched Seraphiel's dim wings.

"And light without rest becomes desperation."

Shadowess moved forward, circling them.

"Every mask you've worn has cracked," she murmured. "Every identity you clung to has shattered."

She leaned close.

"What will you build now?

The same walls?

Or yourselves?"

The quartet trembled.

Not from fear this time — but from truth.

Aurelian opened his eyes in the dark and whispered into the void:

"I am more than strength."

And something heavy was released.

His shoulders dropped. His hands opened, palm-up on his knees, and for the first time in memory, they held nothing — and it was enough.

Zophira breathed unsteadily:

"I am more than clarity."

The fog inside her mind thinned.

Her breath slowed. Her fingers uncurled from fists she hadn't known she was making, and the space behind her eyes softened into something that did not need to understand everything to feel safe.

Solana pressed a hand to her chest:

"I deserve care too."

Warmth pooled inside her.

She pressed both hands to her own chest — not to give, but to hold. The gesture was small and foreign and sacred.

Seraphiel lifted his head, voice fragile but sincere:

"My light belongs to me first."

A soft glow danced in the darkness.

The glow came from somewhere deeper than effort. It rose from his center like heat from embers that had never gone out — steady, unhurried, his.

The river surged — not violently, but with purpose — wrapping around them, holding them, supporting them.

Shadowess smiled faintly.

"Good. Truth is not found by fighting darkness." Celeve placed a hand over each of their hearts. "It is found by meeting yourself where you are." The mire loosened fully.

The quartet felt air again. Light.

The river around them moving gently. They had not risen yet. Not fully.

But they were no longer drowning. They were breathing again.

The river whispered:

"Fall. See. Rise."

And for the first time, the quartet understood Surrender wasn't giving up. It was letting truth in.

Chapter 17: ECHOES OF BALANCE

The Dark Land felt different. Not lighter — but quieter, as if the shadows were watching instead of attacking.

As if the land itself was waiting to see what the quartet would do with the truths, they had finally allowed in.

The quartet moved slowly along the riverbank, each step careful, deliberate. Their bodies were tired, their spirits scraped raw, but beneath the exhaustion was something new:

Not certainty. Not strength. Balance.

The air smelled different here — not clean, not sweet, but honest. Like turned earth after a long drought. Like a room after the argument has ended and the windows have been opened. Their skin still carried the memory of the mire: the way it had pressed against bone, the way it had whispered with the weight of everything they had refused to feel. But their lungs worked. Their eyes adjusted. And the ground beneath their feet, though scarred, held firm.

The River of Process flowed beside them, no longer thrashing in chaos, nor dragging them under. Its dark waters rippled gently, reflecting faint glimmers of silver — a quiet echo of the clarity they had begun to reclaim.

Zophira was the first to speak, her voice soft but steady.

"This stillness… it's different from before."

She brushed her fingers along the river's surface. "It's not numbness. It's… presence."

Aurelian nodded, though his gaze stayed fixed on the shifting horizon.

"I feel the heaviness," he admitted, "but it doesn't own me. It's just… there."

He didn't force courage this time.

He let it be a quiet ember instead of a blazing shield.

Solana crouched near a patch of darkened soil, placing her palms gently on the ground.

"It responds differently now," she murmured.

"Not because it's healed — but because we are meeting it honestly." A small sprout pushed through the cracked earth beneath her touch. Not bright.

Not strong. But alive.

Solana's hand moved instinctively — reaching to tend it, to coax it, to give it something from her own diminished reserves. Then she stopped. Her fingers hovered above the fragile green stem, trembling with the effort of not-doing. She pulled her hand back and pressed it against her own knee instead. The sprout did not need her. It needed the soil it was already in. She let it grow on its own. The gesture was small. But for a woman who had spent her life pouring herself into every wounded thing she touched, it was a revolution.

Seraphiel watched the sprout quietly. "The river isn't rushing," he said. "And neither are we. Maybe… balance isn't motion or stillness. Maybe it's alignment."

His wings remained dimmer than usual — but steady.

He did not try to brighten them. He did not reach for the old blaze that had always announced his presence. He let them be what they were — soft, muted, honest. And for the first time, the dimness did not feel like failure. It felt like truth wearing its own face.

They continued along the river until the land opened into a modest clearing. Here, the ground wasn't twisted or scorched, just barren — waiting.

Solana breathed deeply, letting the air fill her lungs without trying to turn it into warmth.

***

In the Land of Soul

The village felt it before anyone could name it.

Selene was kneeling in her garden, pulling weeds that had grown thick and stubborn during the dark weeks. Her hands worked mechanically, but something in the air made her pause. The breeze carried a scent she had almost forgotten — rain-washed stone, the clean mineral smell of the river running clear.

She sat back on her heels and pressed her palm flat against the soil. It was warmer. Not hot — not urgent — just warmer, the way a hand feels when someone holds it without squeezing.

Elder Myrial stood at the edge of the village square, watching the river. Its surface, which had been dull and sluggish for weeks, caught a single thread of light — brief, silver, gone. But she had seen it. She folded her hands and did not speak. She did not need to. The river was not healed. The land was not restored. But something had shifted in the deep architecture of things, the way a foundation settles after an earthquake — not fixed, but no longer falling.

The miller stepped onto his stoop and looked at the sky as if seeing it for the first time in days. He did not smile. He picked up his ledger and opened it. That was enough.

***

In the Dark Land

"I forgot that healing doesn't happen all at once," she said. "It happens in breaths. In moments."

Zophira glanced at her.

"And in truths we stop running from."

Aurelian sat on a fallen, blackened trunk, feeling its rough bark beneath his hands.

"I thought balance meant holding everything together," he said.

"But maybe it's letting things fall — then deciding what's worth picking up again."

He looked down at his hands — scarred, calloused, empty. He had always measured their value by what they carried. Now they carried nothing. And instead of panic, he felt the weight of the earth beneath him, solid and patient. He pressed his palms flat against the blackened bark and let it hold him for a moment instead of the other way around.

Seraphiel stepped closer to the river, watching its gentle current wind through the clearing like a slow, thoughtful breath.

"Light doesn't have to be bright," he said quietly. "Sometimes… steady is enough."

The land around them shifted subtly — no trembling, no sudden eruptions of shadow, just a soft change in atmosphere. As if the Dark Land itself exhaled.

The air warmed — not much, but enough to notice. A scent rose from the cracked earth, something ancient and mineral, like bedrock exposed after a long erosion. It was not pleasant. It was not comforting. But it was real — the smell of something that had stopped pretending to be anything other than what it was.

The quartet felt it. Not approval.

Not peace. Recognition. Zophira's eyes softened.

"The Dark Land mirrors us," she whispered. "It's not just our wounds — it's our integration."

Aurelian ran a hand along the earth.

"And right now… it sees we're no longer fighting ourselves."

Solana placed her palm over her heart.

"We're finally walking with our shadows instead of against them." The River of Process glowed faintly — just a shimmer of light dancing along the surface, subtle yet unmistakable.

Seraphiel smiled, the expression small but real.

"Maybe that's why the river flows differently. It isn't reacting to us anymore."

He paused, eyes reflecting the faint shimmer.

"It's resonating."

They stood together at the water's edge in a quiet, fragile equilibrium.

Nothing grand. Nothing triumphant.

Just truth. Just breath. Just balance.

For the first time since entering the Dark Land, the quartet didn't brace for another attack.

They simply stood shaken, changed, aligned.

Solana reached out and took Aurelian's hand. Not to heal. Not to give. Just to hold. His fingers closed around hers — not gripping, not guarding. Holding. Zophira placed her hand on Seraphiel's shoulder, and he did not flinch from the touch. For the first time, they stood together without roles — without the healer tending, the warrior shielding, the seer searching, the light blazing. They were simply four people who had been broken open and were learning, breath by breath, what it meant to stand in the space where the breaking had happened.

And the land did not resist them. It followed.

Chapter 18: THE ABYSS BECKONS

The Dark Land grew darker the farther they walked — not like nightfall, but like a truth too deep to name.

The River of Process flowed beside them still, yet its voice had changed again. Not chaotic. Not numb.

Restless.

Its waters churned with an uneasy rhythm, as though the river itself sensed what waited ahead.

Each of them felt the pull differently. Aurelian's muscles locked into a defensive brace — the instinct to shield — but there was nothing to shield against. The emptiness ahead was not a blow; it was an invitation to fall, and his body did not know how to protect against willingness. Zophira's thoughts, usually a rapid cascade of analysis, slowed to a crawl, each thought arriving heavy and reluctant, as though her mind already knew that what waited ahead could not be mapped. Solana pressed her palm against her own sternum, feeling for the warmth she carried for others — and found it dimmer than it had ever been, not extinguished but retreating, as though even compassion knew when to brace. Seraphiel's wings drew inward, pressing against his spine. The glow that usually pulsed outward turned inward too, circling somewhere behind his ribs like a flame protecting itself from wind it could not see.

Aurelian scanned the horizon, muscles taut.

"Something's shifting. The land feels… pulled."

Zophira's eyes narrowed, her awareness sharpening. "Pulled is the right word. It's not leading us." She paused, tasting the air.

"It's drawing us in."

A faint tremor rippled beneath the ground, subtle at first, then stronger

a slow, rolling quake that traveled through the bones rather than the soil.

Solana shivered.

"The river doesn't want to go forward… but it can't turn back either." Seraphiel's wings twitched, their glow flashing with a faint unease. "It's not indecision," he whispered.

"It's inevitability."

The terrain shifted beneath their steps — smooth obsidian-like stone replacing dirt and cracked earth. The color drained from the world until everything was washed in hues of charcoal and ash. Even the air tasted muted.

The deeper they went, the quieter it became.

Within moments, even their footsteps stopped echoing.

Aurelian frowned. "The land feels hollow."

Zophira corrected him softly.

"No. It feels… bottomless."

As they continued forward, the ground sloped sharply downward. The River of Process rushed faster beside them, as though pulled by a force too ancient to fight. Its steady whisper became a rising roar.

Solana clutched her vial, heart pounding.

"Something's ahead. Something massive."

The slope led them to the edge of a vast chasm — a monstrous tear in the heart of the Dark Land.

The river plunged into it violently, cascading into a void so deep that no sound returned. The waterfall roared like the earth itself was screaming.

Seraphiel stepped closer, his wings casting faint light over the abyss.

The light didn't reach the bottom. It simply disappeared.

Aurelian swallowed hard.

"What is this place?"

Zophira's voice was barely more than breath. "The Abyss."

The word trembled in the air. The land shifted in response.

Cracks crawled across the obsidian ground, spiderwebbing beneath their feet. A heavy wind rose from the chasm — not cold or warm, but empty, carrying no scent, no texture, no life.

Solana took an involuntary step back.

"It feels… hungry."

Aurelian felt the hunger as a physical thing — a pull at the center of his chest, as though the Abyss recognized the hollow places where his identity had been built around duty and was reaching for them. Zophira experienced it differently: the emptiness tugged at her thoughts, pulling them apart like thread from a spool, each certainty unraveling into a question she could not rewind. Solana's hands went cold. The hunger bypassed her mind entirely and went straight for the warmth she carried — the heat of tending, the temperature of care — and she felt it draining outward, toward the void, as though the Abyss fed on precisely the thing she gave most freely. Seraphiel felt his wings dim to their lowest glow. The hunger was not for his light but for the need behind it — the desperate, lifelong need to be seen. The Abyss consumed that need like oxygen, and without it his wings had nothing to burn.

The wind grew stronger, pulling at their clothes, their hair, their breath.

Aurelian braced himself, planting his feet firmly.

"We've faced Shadowess. Celeve. Fearmonger. The Void. All of them." He exhaled slowly. "This is different."

Zophira nodded.

"Those were fragments. This… is origin."

The River of Process surged suddenly, thrashing against its banks as if resisting the fall into the chasm. Spray hit the quartet's faces — cold, stinging, desperate.

Solana reached out toward the water instinctively.

"It doesn't want this," she whispered. "It's terrified."

Seraphiel shook his head.

"No. Not terrified." His wings dimmed. "Resigned."

The earth trembled again — harder this time — followed by a deep, resonant hum that vibrated in their bones.

The abyss was waking.

Aurelian stepped forward cautiously. "We need to cross." Before anyone could question, the air thickened — so suddenly it felt like the land inhaled.

A massive figure rose from within the chasm — not climbing, not crawling but emerging as though it had always been part of the void itself. Darkness folded into shape. Shadows condensed. The land bowed beneath the weight of its presence.

A voice rolled through the chasm — deep, ancient, and resonant, as though spoken from the marrow of creation itself.

***

Nyxalia

I am the echo of every unspoken truth."

The void shivered at the name. The figure towered above them, amorphous and shifting — never one shape, never one color, never fully solid. It was absence given form, emptiness made visible.

"Guardian of the Abyss. Keeper of the Void Within." Zophira felt her jaw lock. She had seen fear, confusion, anger, numbness — but this? These were truths unspoken.

Nyxalia's gaze — if it could be called that — turned upon them. "You have walked far. But distance is not depth." Aurelian's breath caught. "What do you want from us?"

Nyxalia's form pulsed, the shadows rippling outward. "Not what I want. What you don't say — the necessary truths you refuse to speak and the things you avoid."

The ground beneath them cracked again — thin fissures radiating outward like veins of darkness.

Solana's voice trembled. "We all care!" The abyss rumbled, a sound both mocking and mournful.

"All souls say they care. Do you?" Seraphiel spread his wings, though their glow dimmed under Nyxalia's presence. "We came to face whatever lies within."

Nyxalia's voice sharpened. "Then face this." The void surged upward, swirling around them, pulling at their bodies and hearts. "The final truth is not only the balance of light and shadow; it is the void left by truths you refuse to speak — silence that makes you complicit."

The quartet stiffened as Nyxalia's words dug beneath their skin. Zophira whispered, "It's not attacking us." Seraphiel swallowed. "No." His eyes widened. "It's unveiling us."

Nyxalia drew closer, the void stretching into a vast, all-consuming presence. "You cannot cross the abyss," it intoned, "until you face the void within." The ground buckled. The darkness surged. The river screamed.

The chapter closes with the quartet standing at the precipice — the Abyss before them, Nyxalia rising, the void inside them stirring awake.

Chapter 19: THE ABYSS WITHIN

Darkness wrapped around them in a living shroud — not an absence of light, but a presence of shadow so absolute it felt like the land was breathing against their skin.

The Abyss throbbed beneath their feet. Nyxalia towered above them, not solid, not phantom — a shifting mass of void that pulsed with their heartbeats. The River of Process raged at the edge of the chasm, its waters a storm of light and shadow, as though even the river feared what would come next.

Nyxalia's voice resonated from everywhere and nowhere at once. "You stand at the edge of truth. You have faced your shadows. Now face your emptiness."

Aurelian felt the ground tilt beneath him — not physically, but inside his chest. Courage flickered. Breath faltered.

"What… do you mean?" he forced out.

Nyxalia lowered toward them, its form bending the air as though gravity itself bowed to it. "Fear. Anger. Doubt. Confusion. All are echoes. All are surface." A pulse rippled through the void. "But beneath them lies your deepest terror: a hollow place inside you that nothing can fill."

The words hit like a blow. The land went silent. Aurelian's knees trembled. Solana's chest constricted. Zophira's vision blurred. Seraphiel's wings collapsed inward.

Nyxalia turned its shifting gaze toward Aurelian first.

***

Aurelian

The air thickened around him — tightening, compressing, like invisible hands gripping his ribs. He gasped. The void wrapped around his chest and pulled something forward: a memory, a moment, a truth he had never let himself look at. He saw himself as a child — alone, standing beside someone he had once tried to save and could not. He had carried that moment for years as if it were an oath carved into his bones.

Nyxalia whispered, "Your courage was born from emptiness. A need to matter. To prove you were enough."

Aurelian choked. "That's not… that's not true—"

"Is it not?" Nyxalia pressed deeper. "Every moment you protected others, was it only love? Or a desperate attempt to silence the hollow where you felt unworthy?"

His breath broke. His chest caved inward. Tears burned behind his eyes. He whispered into the void, voice cracking like shattered stone: "I… I didn't want to be nothing."

The words unleashed a tremor through the chasm. Nyxalia's presence softened for a moment. "Then stop trying to fill the emptiness with others. Let the space be yours."

Aurelian collapsed forward — not in defeat, but in the first step toward truth.

***

Zophira

The void shifted toward Zophira next, curling around her mind like smoke that knew her thoughts before she thought them. Her clarity flickered. Her breathing quickened. Nyxalia's voice vibrated through her skull. "You seek truth to avoid yourself."

Zophira recoiled. "That's not— I'm trying to understand—"

"Yes," the void agreed. "But not out of wisdom. Out of fear that if you are not the one who knows, you will be nothing."

Her vision fractured — dozens of mirrored reflections, each one showing a version of her searching, striving, reaching — alone. She pressed her shaking hands to her head. "I just wanted to help—"

"By anchoring yourself to answers," Nyxalia murmured, "because you do not know who you are without them."

Her breath hitched. Her voice dropped to a trembling whisper: "I don't. I don't know who I am if I am not the one who sees clearly." Then, softly, like a truth blooming in darkness: "And that frightens me."

Nyxalia dipped its head to her. "Then surrender clarity. Let yourself be unknown."

A tear slipped down her cheek as she nodded slowly.

***

Solana

The void leaned close to Solana, feeling her pulse, her breath, the trembling of her ribs. "Your light has been a gift," Nyxalia whispered. "But also a refuge. A mask to hide the emptiness you never tended."

Her lip quivered. "I wasn't hiding — I was helping—"

"You were giving," the void corrected. "Because receiving felt dangerous."

Solana froze. No Shadow had ever spoken this truth aloud. Nyxalia pressed deeper. "You healed others so you would not have to feel your own longing."

She shook her head violently. "No — no, I—" But the truth rose anyway, breaking through the walls she had built so carefully. "I didn't know how to be loved," she whispered. "I only knew how to give."

Her knees buckled. Nyxalia's voice softened. "Then let the emptiness ache. Let love find the space you have never allowed."

Solana pressed a hand to her heart as something inside her cracked open — raw, tender, real.

***

Seraphiel

Nyxalia towered over Seraphiel last. His wings, usually bright even when dimmed, hung limp at his sides. The void coiled around him, holding him in a cocoon of darkness. "You shine for the world," Nyxalia said quietly, "but not for yourself."

Seraphiel's breath trembled. His throat closed. "I shine because someone has to." "You shine," the void interrupted, "because you fear the darkness you carry. Not the world's. Yours."

His knees shook. No one had ever spoken this to him. No one had ever dared. Nyxalia's voice vibrated through the marrow of his wings. "Your deepest fear is not that your light will go out. Your fear is that without your light — you are nothing."

The words broke something inside him he didn't know could break. His voice cracked, guttural and soft: "I don't want to disappear."

The void trembled — as if acknowledging pain, it understood intimately. "Then stop shining for survival. Shine for truth."

Seraphiel lowered his head — not in defeat, but in revelation.

***

The Moment of Surrender

Nyxalia rose tall again, its presence vast, ancient, and strangely tender. "You have faced your shadows. But today, you faced yourselves." The ground shook. The river surged. The abyss pulsed with a new rhythm — the rhythm of awakening.

Nyxalia's voice deepened: "The void inside you is not your enemy. It is a space — waiting for truth. It is the space carved out by your unspoken truths — the quiet that feeds the darkness."

The quartet stood, trembling, hearts shattered open. Not broken. Open. Nyxalia withdrew slightly. The darkness loosened. The void around them shifted, no longer suffocating — spacious. Inviting.

"Rise," Nyxalia said. Its voice was no longer a test. It was a blessing. "You are ready."

Chapter 20: THE GATHERING STORM

The River of Process flowed differently now.

Not wild as before, not numb as in the beginning — but steady, pulsing with a deeper rhythm, as though it recognized the quartet's transformation and responded in kind.

The land around them felt neither hostile nor welcoming. It simply was.

Bare. Honest. Waiting.

The quartet walked in silence for a long time — not because they feared speaking, but because the truths revealed in the Abyss were still settling inside them.

Every step felt like a fragile agreement with the earth beneath their feet: We will carry what we have seen.

We will not turn away from it now. Aurelian was the first to break the silence. "I feel… different," he said quietly.

He didn't sound proud or ashamed — just sincere.

"It's like something inside me cracked open. And it hasn't closed."

Zophira nodded gently.

"It's not supposed to."

She did not look at him when she spoke.

Her eyes traced the river's shifting reflections.

"When truth breaks us, the pieces have to rearrange before we become whole again."

Aurelian breathed out — a soft, unguarded sound.

"Then I guess I'm not in a hurry to fix myself."

Solana smiled faintly, though her eyes carried a depth the others hadn't

seen in her before.

"Maybe that's the healing," she whispered. "Not rushing to be whole.

But learning to be honest with the broken pieces." Seraphiel walked behind them, wings folded loosely. He said nothing, but his silence was no longer the silence of pressure — the silence of holding himself together for others.

This silence felt like space. Room.

Zophira watched him for a moment. "You're quiet," she said softly.

Seraphiel inhaled as though the air was thicker than usual. His voice came slowly, tender.

"It's strange," he admitted. "For the first time...

I feel my light without needing it to be bright."

The others turned.

Seraphiel's wings glowed faintly — not radiant, not dim, but steady. "I always thought my purpose was to shine for others," he continued, "to guide, to illuminate, to carry everyone else forward in the dark." He looked at his hands — not in shame, but with new recognition. "But now... I feel like I'm finally shining for me."

The river shimmered briefly at his words — a soft acknowledgement. Solana moved closer and placed a hand on his arm.

"That light feels different," she said. "More honest."

He nodded.

The land responded to their unity with small, almost imperceptible changes: a patch of dried moss softening, a dying branch regaining color, the faint sound of wind returning to a space that had been airless for too long.

It was not healing fast — but healing honestly.

Aurelian slowed his steps as the terrain leveled out, revealing a wide stretch of quiet plain. He scanned the landscape with an instinct that was no longer fueled by fear, but awareness.

"Something's coming," he said.

Zophira closed her eyes briefly, listening with her mind.

"Yes. The darkness isn't chasing us anymore." Solana added, "But it's not gone."

Seraphiel stepped beside them, wings extending slightly. "It's waiting."

The wind shifted — barely noticeable, but enough to brush against their skin like a warning.

Not sharp. Not cold. Not violent.

Just… aware.

The land held its breath.

The river pulsed more rapidly. Aurelian placed a hand over his heart.

"We're not in danger," he said slowly, "but we're not finished." "No," Zophira agreed.

"This is the stillness before truth settles.

Not peace — transition."

Solana's hand glowed faintly as she touched the ground. "The land is watching us," she whispered.

"Feeling what we feel."

Seraphiel looked toward the horizon, where the shadows gathered in a thick, unmoving wall.

Not closing in — simply standing there, as if waiting to be invited.

"The final test isn't outside us," he murmured. "It never was."

Zophira nodded.

"The final test is living with the truths we saw."

Aurelian straightened his posture — not rigidly, but with a quiet resolve that came from within, not from expectation.

"Then we meet it," he said.

The wind stirred again, this time with purpose.

The river surged — not violently, but with determination, as if urging them forward.

The land vibrated with subtle tension — a low hum that crawled through the soil into the soles of their feet.

Solana stood and walked to the river's edge.

She traced a hand through the water.

"We've surrendered," she whispered. "We've fallen." Zophira stepped beside her. "And now we walk in truth." Aurelian joined them.

"And in balance."

Seraphiel lifted his wings, their glow steady.

"And in light — the kind that begins inside."

Together, they looked ahead.

The path was not twisted or shifting anymore.

It was straight — eerily, unnervingly straight — cutting through the last region of the Dark Land and vanishing into a horizon that trembled with shadow.

Zophira's voice was soft:

"It's time." Aurelian nodded. Solana exhaled.

Seraphiel's wings unfurled.

They stepped forward together.

And behind them, the river flowed in quiet solidarity — a reflection of every truth they carried now.

***

Aftermath: Village Ritual

When the dust settled, the village gathered at dusk in the square and to make meaning of what had been lost and what remained; not as victors but as people who had been given back a small, fragile thing: the right to breathe without immediate fear. Lanterns swung low, their light pooled like careful hands. The villagers moved with a slow, ceremonial quiet — not the noisy relief of celebration but the careful tending of something that might still be raw.

Maelis stood near the loom she had brought from the market, a strip of cloth already threaded with river knots and tiny jasmines. She had sewn a dozen small talismans the night before; now she handed them out with fingers that trembled only a little. "For remembering," she said to each person, and the words landed like a stitch.

Elder Myrial took the center of the circle and spoke in the voice that had once steadied a child at the riverbank. "We name what we have lost and what we have kept," she said. "We do not pretend the cost is small. We only refuse to let it be the last word." Her hands moved in a slow, practiced pattern, and the villagers echoed her with a soft, communal breath.

Solana moved among them with bowls of warm broth, offering a ladle and a steady hand. She knelt by the child who had nearly been taken by the river and pressed a cloth to his forehead, humming the same low tune she used at dawn. The child's small fingers curled around hers, and for a moment the world narrowed to the simple exchange of warmth.

Aurelian stood at the edge of the circle, not apart but watchful. When a young man approached with a splintered oar and a face that had not yet learned to smile, Aurelian took the oar and set it upright in the earth like a marker. "We mark what we have crossed," he said, voice low. "We remember the stones that held and the ones that broke." The man nodded, and something like relief loosened in his shoulders.

Zophira braided the length of river reed into a small crown and placed it on the head of the village's eldest fisherwoman. "So, the tide remembers to return," she murmured. The fisherwoman's eyes shone; she pressed the crown to her chest as if it were a map she could carry.

Seraphiel moved through the crowd with a sprig of jasmine, touching it to foreheads and palms. "For witness," they said softly. "So, we do not carry alone." Each touch left a scent that lingered like a promise.

When the ritual reached its quiet center, the villagers formed a ring and spoke names aloud — not a litany of blame but a ledger of memory: the lost, the saved, the small mercies. Each name was answered with a single clap, a sound that stitched the circle tighter. The claps were uneven at first, then steadier, until the rhythm itself felt like a small, communal heartbeat.

Afterward they shared bread and broth, passing bowls and stories. The talk was practical — who would mend the bridge, who would watch the ford at dawn — and it was tender: a woman telling of a child's laugh, a boy offering to fetch more wood. The work of repair began in the ordinary ways: hands that could sew, feet that could carry, eyes that could watch.

Before they left, Elder Myrial lifted her hand. "Tonight we named and tended," she said. "Tomorrow we will begin the slow work of rebuilding. Not only the bridge, but the trust that lets us cross it together."

They dispersed into the night with small talismans tucked into pockets and the jasmine scent clinging to their clothes. The ritual had not erased the river's lesson, but it had given them a way to carry it — together, with hands that remembered how to hold.

Chapter 21: LIGHT WITHIN THE SHADOWS

The Dark Land shuddered beneath them — not violently, but with a deep, resonant rumble that vibrated through the ground like a warning.

The path ahead narrowed, and the River of Process flowed slower, as though reluctant to continue.

Aurelian paused.

"This feels… different." Solana's fingers brushed the air.

"It's thick. Like the shadows are gathering." Zophira scanned the terrain with new, deeper sight. "It's not a threat. It's a shift."

Seraphiel's wings lifted slightly. "A choice."

Before anyone could respond, the earth cracked beneath their feet.

A roar of wind whipped around them — cold, sharp, spiraling — and walls of black stone burst from the ground, cutting through the land like jagged knives. Seraphiel reached for Solana's hand, but the walls shot upward, sealing them off.

Solana's voice echoed faintly, "Aurelian? Seraphiel? Zophira!"

Aurelian slammed his fists against the stone.

"Stay calm! We'll—"

The walls trembled.

A low, ancient hum surged through them. And the labyrinth awakened.

AURELIAN

The corridor around him tightened, narrowing like a throat.

Aurelian inhaled carefully, forcing himself to breathe past the rising tension.

"You again?"

The voice slithered from the dark ahead. Not mocking.

Not cruel.

But familiar.

Fearmonger stepped out of the shadows — not as monstrous as before, but more… personal. More human, even.

"You faced the void," Fearmonger said softly. "But courage is not found once." It leaned closer.

"You must choose it again. And again. And again." Aurelian's jaw tightened.

"I'm not afraid of you anymore." "Oh," Fearmonger whispered, "But you're afraid of yourself." The walls around him shook.

Stone cracked. Dust rained down.

Aurelian's body tensed — not out of fear, but realization.

He remembered every time he had thrown himself between someone and harm — not because they asked, but because standing still felt like dying. His shoulders carried the ghost of every impact, every blow absorbed on someone else's behalf. The muscles remembered even when the mind tried to forget. And here, in this narrowing corridor, with no one to shield, his body did not know what to do with itself. His hands opened and closed at his sides, reaching for a weight that was not there. The absence of a threat felt more disorienting than any shadow he had faced.

Fearmonger didn't block his path. It waited.

Aurelian stepped forward slowly.

"I don't need to defeat you," he said.

"I need to walk with what you show me."

Fearmonger bowed its head.

"You finally see."

The corridor opened.

ZOPHIRA

Mist curled along her corridor, thick and shifting. But this time, she didn't rush to see through it.

She let it breathe. Let it exist.

Perplexia materialized ahead — shapeshifting in erratic, dizzying spirals.

"You can't trust what you see!" it cried.

"You can't trust what you think! You can't—" "I know," Zophira whispered.

Perplexia froze. Her eyes softened.

"I know I can't trust everything. Because I'm not meant to."

She took a steady breath.

Her mind had always been a cathedral of maps — corridors of logic branching into corridors of analysis, every doorway labeled, every passage measured. She had built it that way on purpose, stone by stone, because the alternative was a world without edges, and a world without edges was a world where she could disappear. She remembered the first-time clarity had failed her — not a dramatic collapse, but a quiet erosion. A question she couldn't answer. A pattern that refused to resolve. The vertigo of standing in her own mind and finding a room she hadn't built. Her fingers, still now at her sides, remembered the frantic motion of reaching for a pen, a chart, a frame — anything to hold the world in place. Here in this mist, with nothing to map, she felt that vertigo again. But this time she did not reach.

"I'm meant to discern — not perfect. Not control.

Not know everything.," The mist lifted.

A path cleared.

Perplexia dissolved.

Zophira walked forward with clearer sight than she had ever possessed.

SOLANA

Her corridor felt colder than the others — quiet, echoing, empty. She stepped carefully, cradling her vial close, expecting an attack. But instead—

The Apathetic Void emerged, shape sagging like a half-formed shadow struggling to stand.

"You give because you fear you are not enough," it murmured. "Without your healing, who are you?"

Solana swallowed. Her voice trembled, but her heart did not.

She thought of every bedside she had sat beside, every forehead she had cooled, every wound she had dressed while her own hands ached. She remembered the precise moment she had learned to make her exhaustion invisible — a skill no one had asked for but everyone had come to depend on. Her body knew the posture of perpetual availability: shoulders angled toward whoever needed her, weight shifted to her front foot, hands already reaching before the request was spoken. In this cold corridor, with no one to tend, her body defaulted to that posture anyway — leaning forward, hands extended toward empty air. The ache in her wrists was real. The habit of reaching was so deep it lived in her bones. And the Void's question landed not as an attack but as an honest mirror: without the reaching, what shape was she?

"I'm learning," she said.

"That I don't have to earn love by giving it.

That I can rest.

That I can be held."

Her vial glowed faintly — a warm pulse that expanded outward. The Void stepped back, its edges softening.

"You are becoming whole," it whispered. "And I am no longer needed."

The corridor brightened with gentle, golden light. Solana stepped forward, tears warm on her cheeks.

SERAPHIEL

His corridor was pitch black. No sound.

No movement.

He extended his wing to guide himself — but the darkness swallowed even his light.

A whisper rose behind him. Not a shadow.

Not Nyxalia. His own voice.

"If no one can see your light…, do you still believe it's there?"

Seraphiel froze.

The darkness thickened around him, like a hand closing around his heart.

He had spent his life answering that question with performance — brighter, higher, more visible. Every room he entered, he lit. Every silence, he filled with radiance. He remembered the first time someone had looked away from his glow, and he had felt not relief but panic — a cold, chest-deep certainty that without the light he was nothing anyone would choose to stay for. His wings had learned to compensate brighter when he was tired, steadier when he was afraid, warmer when he was hollow. The muscle memory of performance lived in the joints where wing met spine — a constant low-grade tension he had mistaken for purpose. Here in the absolute dark, that tension had nothing to push against. His wings hung heavy and still, and the weight of them without their function felt like grief.

He swallowed hard. Closed his eyes, searched his heart and whispered:

"Yes."

Light surged — not from around him, but from within him — soft at first, then steady, then radiant.

The darkness shuddered, then peeled away like old skin. His wings illuminated the corridor in warm, white light. And the path opened.

***

REUNITING

The walls around them began to tremble — not collapsing, but receding, melting into the earth as though they had served their purpose.

The quartet stepped into the same clearing at once. Aurelian — strong, centered.

Zophira — clear-eyed, grounded. Solana — soft, steady, luminous. Seraphiel — radiant, authentic.

A moment of silence passed. Then Seraphiel smiled. "You all look… different." Solana laughed softly.

"Feels different."

The ground shook softly beneath them — but not in warning. In acknowledgment.

A gentle wind rose, brushing their faces like a blessing.

Zophira looked toward the horizon where the Dark Land thinned, giving way to distant light.

"The final trial is close," she said. "But this time, we're walking in truth— not fear."

Aurelian nodded. "In unity — not roles." Solana lifted her vial, now shining from within. "With open hearts — not empty ones."

Seraphiel's wings flared brightly.

"With light that belongs to us — not the world's expectations."

Together, they stepped forward. The land did not resist them.

It opened.

Chapter 22: THE DARK LAND'S RECKONING

The River of Process thundered beside them — not with the chaos of earlier trials, but with a force that felt deliberate, ancient, awakened.

The river was no longer reflecting the land. It was responding to it — as though both realms, Soul and Shadow, were converging toward a single fate.

The air tasted of iron and memory — every trial, every shadow, every wound they had walked through now pressing against their skin like weather. Aurelian felt it in his shoulders first, the familiar weight of carrying, but different now. Not a burden placed on him. A gravity that belonged to the land itself, pulling everything toward its center.

Aurelian watched the surging water with steady eyes.

"It's stronger," he murmured. "Not wild. Strong."

Zophira listened, head tilted.

"It's carrying something," she said. "A message."

Solana knelt and touched the river.

The water flared with light around her fingertips — light braided with shadow. She gasped softly.

The sensation traveled up her arm — not pain, but recognition. She had felt this before, in the Hollowshade's numbing silence, in the Wrathbearer's furnace heat, in every trial that had stripped something from her. But the river wasn't stripping now. It was returning. Every emotion she had surrendered to survive was flowing back, braided together — grief and tenderness, exhaustion and fierce, stubborn love.

"It's reflecting us," she whispered. "Our truth. Our changes."

Seraphiel stepped closer, his wings shimmering a radiant silver-gold.

"The Dark Land is not just reacting to us anymore," he said slowly. "It's aligning."

The ground rumbled beneath them — not violently, but with intention. Like the heartbeat of a world preparing for rebirth.

Aurelian planted his feet and let the tremor move through him instead of bracing against it. His bones hummed with the frequency. Zophira closed her eyes, and for the first time in the Dark Land, she did not try to read the pattern. She let it read her. Seraphiel's wings caught the vibration and amplified it — not with his own light, but with something older, something the land was lending him.

A low wind swept across the landscape, stirring dust and shadow into spiraling streams. The land trembled in waves, as if exhaling tension it had held for centuries.

Zophira's eyes widened. "It's beginning.

The reckoning."

Aurelian turned toward her. "What reckoning?"

She pointed to the horizon.

The shadows were thinning — not dispersing, not dying, but pulling inward, gathering into a concentrated mass at the center of the Dark Land.

As if every fragment of fear, doubt, anger, numbness, confusion —

every shadow they had faced — was returning to its source.

Aurelian recognized the Wrathbearer's heat threading through the mass — the same fire that had once tried to consume him from the inside. Beside it, the Shadowkeeper's weighted presence, the Fearmonger's sharp-edged whisper, the Hollowshade's terrible quiet. Each shadow he had faced was still itself, still distinct, but no longer hunting. They were going home.

Zophira watched the convergence with tears she didn't try to explain. Every fragment of confusion Perplexia had scattered through her thoughts, every false certainty she had clung to — she could feel them gathering, not into answers, but into a question large enough to hold the truth.

Solana pressed both hands against her chest. The emptiness the Apathetic Void had opened in her was still there — she understood now that it would always be there. But it was no longer a wound. It was a room. A space inside her that could hold grief without being consumed by it.

Seraphiel felt Nyxalia's darkness pass through him like a shudder — the raw, annihilating emptiness that had nearly swallowed his light in the Abyss. But his wings did not dim. The darkness moved through him and continued, joining the convergence, and he remained. Whole. Not because his light had conquered the dark, but because he had stopped asking it to.

The land shuddered again. Solana steadied herself against Aurelian's arm.

"It feels like the land is preparing… for something immense." Seraphiel's wings twitched.

"It's not preparing," he said softly. "It's remembering."

The sky rippled — like a veil being drawn aside.

And the river responded, surging forward in one massive wave that cascaded across the plains, illuminating the land in brilliant streaks of gold and silver.

The quartet shielded their eyes.

When the light faded, they saw a pathway carved through the shadows — straight, unwavering, leading into the heart of the Dark Land.

Aurelian's breath steadied. "That wasn't an accident."

Zophira nodded.

"The river is guiding us.

To where everything leads." Solana's voice trembled with awe. "The final convergence." Seraphiel lifted his wings.

"Then we follow."

***

Meanwhile, in the Land of Soul…

The River of Process surged with the same force — flooding its banks, rippling through fields and gardens, carrying light into every corner of the village.

Villagers gasped, staring as the once-wounded water now blazed with silver-gold fire.

The baker's apprentice dropped his flour sack at the river's edge, watching the golden current sweep past the mill wheel. The weaver abandoned her loom mid-thread, drawn to the window by a hum she felt in her teeth. Children who had been warned away from the river for weeks now stood at its banks, mouths open, unafraid for the first time since the shadows had begun to bleed through.

Selene, hands trembling, whispered:

"They're doing something… I can feel it."

Doran shielded his eyes.

"The river hasn't glowed like this in my lifetime."

Elder Myrial stood at the water's edge, heart pounding with recognition.

"This is not a warning," she said. "This is awakening." Elder Tovrik stepped beside her. "The quartet is near the source." "They are," Myrial whispered.

"They've begun the reckoning the land could not complete on its own."

Tovrik placed a weathered hand on Myrial's shoulder. Neither of them spoke for a long moment. They had carried the village through weeks of dimming light and creeping fear, rationing hope the way others rationed grain.

"I was not sure they would make it this far," Tovrik said quietly. "I was not sure we would."

Myrial covered his hand with hers. "We held the ground. They walked the dark. Neither could have done the other's work."

Around them, the village stirred with a different energy — not the frantic motion of fear, but the slow, deliberate movement of people remembering how to trust. A farmer knelt by the irrigation channel, watching the golden water fill it. A mother lifted her child to see the river's glow, and the child laughed — a sound so ordinary it felt like a miracle.

A hush swept through the villagers as the ground beneath their feet hummed with a deep, resonant chord.

A chord of unity. A chord of truth.

For the first time in weeks — maybe years — fear did not dominate the square.

Hope did.

***

Back in the Dark Land

The quartet stepped onto the new path formed by the river's surge.

The shadows trembled around them, as if bowing in acknowledgment. Every step forward caused the ground to ripple with light — faint,

flickering, but undeniable.

Solana pressed a hand over her heart.

"Do you feel it?" Aurelian nodded. "Yes."

Zophira exhaled slowly.

"The land is shifting with us."

Seraphiel gazed toward the horizon, where the shadows converged into a spiraling vortex.

"No," he whispered.

"We are shifting with it."

The realization settled into each of them differently. For Aurelian, it was the absence of the need to lead — the path that existed, and he could walk it without forging it. For Zophira, it was the relief of a question that did not require her answer. For Solana, it was the strange warmth of being carried by something she had not tended or healed. For Seraphiel, it was the discovery that his wings could catch a current he had created and that riding it felt nothing like surrender. It felt like trust.

Thunder rumbled in the depths of the earth. The air vibrated with tension.

The river pulsed like a second heartbeat beside them. Aurelian clenched his fists — not in fear, but in readiness. "This is it."

Zophira's eyes sharpened.

"The reckoning is not just for the land."

Solana inhaled, a tremor of anticipation running through her.

"It's for us."

Seraphiel's wings expanded, brightening the path ahead.

"Then let's meet it as the selves we've become — not the selves we once was."

Together, they stepped forward into the gathering storm. And the Dark Land opened.

Chapter 23: BECOMING THE LIGHT

The Dark Land had gone quiet.

Not empty. Not finished. Quiet in the way a held breath waits for release.

The River of Process flowed beside the quartet, its surface dimmer now— not wounded, but restrained, as if conserving its strength. The land bore the marks of everything they had endured: fractured stone, scorched soil, shadows lingering like memories that refused to fade.

Aurelian's hands hung at his sides, open and scarred. Zophira stood with her gaze level — not searching, not calculating, just present. Solana's palms rested against her own ribs, feeling the steady pulse beneath. Seraphiel's wings held their quiet glow, neither straining for brilliance nor folding in retreat. They had not slept. They had not eaten. But something in them had settled into a frequency that did not require rest — only honesty.

They had crossed the trials. They had survived the reckoning. And yet—

Aurelian broke the silence, his voice low. "We faced the land. We faced ourselves." His gaze swept the horizon. "So why does it feel like we're standing still?"

Solana knelt at the river's edge, her fingers slipping into the cold current. A faint shimmer stirred beneath her touch, but it did not rise. She withdrew her hand slowly. "Because we only changed when we had no choice," she said. "We reacted. We endured. But we haven't chosen who we are."

The words hung in the air like smoke. Aurelian looked at her, and for the first time did not reach for reassurance or resolution. He let the truth sit. Zophira closed her eyes and felt the weight of every pattern she had ever mapped — every crisis she had charted, every danger she had named before it arrived. All of it had been reaction. Brilliant, necessary reaction; But reaction, nonetheless.

Seraphiel's wings shifted, their glow steady but muted. "Understanding isn't transformation," he said. "We learned who we could be — but only in moments of crisis."

Zophira's eyes sharpened with recognition. "Knowing the truth isn't the same as living it."

The land trembled — just once. Not a warning. An invitation.

Solana felt it in the soles of her feet — a deep, slow vibration that rose through her ankles, her knees, her hips. Not the violent shaking of collapse but something older; Something patient. Like the earth asking a question it had been holding for a long time.

She hesitated. Not from doubt — from the sheer enormity of what it meant to choose. To stop surviving and start becoming. Her hands trembled. Her breath caught. For a moment, she stood at the edge of the only kind of cliff that truly terrifies: the one where you jump not away from something, but toward yourself.

Aurelian saw her hesitate. He did not encourage her. He did not offer strength or a steady hand. He simply stepped forward first — not leading, not rescuing, just moving. His step was not dramatic. It was the most ordinary thing in the world: one foot, then the other, into the space where fear used to live.

And Solana followed. Not because he led. Because his step gave her permission to take her own.

Zophira moved next, her jaw set with something fiercer than clarity — conviction. Seraphiel came last, and as he stepped forward, his wings flared — not bright, but warm. The glow came from his center, not his effort.

Solana stood, her voice gaining strength. "We've been waiting for the land to heal." She looked at each of them in turn. "But it's been waiting for us."

Aurelian's shoulders squared. "Then the first step isn't forward." He exhaled. "It's inward."

Seraphiel stepped ahead, wings flaring brighter. "Then we stop bracing for impact." His light intensified. "We become what we've learned."

They moved. Not cautiously. Not defensively. With intention. Aurelian's steps were grounded, each one a declaration of presence rather than resistance.

His shoulders ached — a deep, physical ache that had nothing to do with exhaustion and everything to do with the cost of becoming. Transformation was not painless. His muscles remembered every shield he had carried, and now they trembled with the effort of holding nothing at all. But the trembling was honest, and he let it be.

Zophira walked beside him, clarity guiding her gaze — not searching for danger but choosing direction.

Her breath came in sharp, deliberate pulls. Each step felt like a sentence she was writing with her body — precise, intentional, and for the first time, not a response to someone else's crisis but a declaration of her own direction.

Seraphiel's light no longer pushed back the darkness; it illuminated the path as though it had always belonged there.

Solana trailed her fingers along the earth. Where she touched, the land responded. Cracks softened.

Green pierced the soil.

Withered branches stirred, buds forming where none should have survived.

Her breath caught. "It's listening."

"Yes," Zophira said quietly. "It's also mirroring."

The River of Process surged — not violently, but purposefully — its glow strengthened as it flowed straighter, clearer, unbroken.

***

In the Land of Soul

The change was immediate.

The River brightened, silver-gold light spilling across its banks. Villagers gathered, gasping as warmth spread through the fields. Fear loosened its grip, replaced by something unfamiliar — resolve.

Selene pressed a hand to her chest. "They're not fighting anymore."

Elder Myrial watched the water with reverent stillness. "They're leading by being."

Tovrik emerged from the council hall, his weathered face drawn but watchful. He stood beside Myrial and said nothing for a long moment. Then, quietly: "The river hasn't looked like this since before the trembling started." He pressed his palm flat against the nearest post as if testing whether the world was still solid. It was. The wood was warm beneath his hand.

A young woman — the blacksmith's apprentice — set down her hammer and walked to the river's edge. She knelt and cupped the water in both hands. It shimmered. She did not drink it. She simply held it, watching the light move, then let it fall back. "It's clear," she said to no one in particular. "It's actually clear."

***

In the Dark Land

The shadows attempted to rise — but found no anchor. There was nothing to cling to.

No hesitation. No fracture.

Solana knelt once more, pressing both palms to the ground. Light surged outward.

Wildflowers erupted across the barren plain, color spilling where gray had ruled. The river flared brilliantly beside them, its current steady and sure.

Aurelian turned to her, awe softening his voice. "You're restoring it."
She looked up, eyes shining. "We are."

Aurelian knelt beside her, pressing his own hands into the soil. Light did not surge from him — that was not his gift. But the ground beneath his palms steadied, firmed, as though his presence alone was enough to remind the earth what it was made of. Zophira stood at the river's edge, watching its current with eyes that no longer searched for threat but traced the shape of what was emerging. "The pattern is changing," she said. Not with alarm. With wonder. Seraphiel lifted his wings and let the glow fall across the plain like late afternoon sun — unhurried, generous, asking nothing in return.

They moved as one now — no pauses, no doubt. Their gifts flowed freely, not summoned by fear but guided by choice. The land reshaped itself around them, not because it was commanded, but because it recognized them.

The River of Process stretched ahead, luminous and unwavering.

And for the first time since entering the Dark Land, the quartet understood:

The light was never something they were meant to reach. It was something they were meant to be.

Chapter 24: THE CIRCLE OF LIGHT

The River of Process flowed as if it had reached an understanding.

Its waters no longer gurgled or strained. They moved with quiet certainty, luminous and whole, threading through the Land of Soul like a vow fulfilled. The quartet stood at its edge, breathing in the stillness — not the stillness of exhaustion, but of arrival.

Behind them, the Dark Land rested. Not erased. Not denied. Integrated.

Aurelian could still feel the mire's weight in his joints — a phantom heaviness that would take time to fade. He did not try to shake it off. It belonged to him now, not as burden but as record. Zophira carried a quiet behind her eyes that was new — not the silence of exhaustion, but the silence of someone who had finally stopped narrating the world and started living in it. Solana walked with her hands at her sides, fingers uncurled. It was the most radical posture she had ever held: a healer with empty hands and no one to tend. Seraphiel's wings caught the amber light and held it without amplifying it. He let the glow be what it was — borrowed, brief, enough.

Its shadows no longer pressed against the horizon. They lingered softly, like memories that had been faced and honored. The land no longer resisted their presence. It recognized them.

They walked until the river widened and the land opened into a clearing bathed in warm, amber light. Here, something within them asked for pause — not to stop, but to acknowledge.

Seraphiel coaxed a small fire into being its flames steady and calm. They gathered around it, forming a circle — not out of necessity, but completion.

The flames moved without urgency, painting their faces in warm, shifting copper. For a long moment, no one spoke. The silence was not awkward or expectant — it was the kind of quiet that comes after a long journey, when the body finally believes it has arrived. Aurelian sat with his elbows on his knees, hands loose between them. Not guarding. Not gripping. Just resting. Solana leaned back and looked up at the sky — the first time in weeks she had looked at anything without calculating what it needed from her. The stars were steady and indifferent and beautiful. Zophira traced a pattern in the dirt with her fingertip — not a map, not a plan, just the absent, contented motion of someone whose mind had finally gone quiet. Seraphiel watched the fire and let himself be warmed by something he had not created. That alone felt like a homecoming.

Zophira watched the fire dance. "I thought the trials were the end," she said quietly. "That once we faced the shadows, the land would finally be at peace."

Aurelian nodded, his voice grounded. "I thought strength meant enduring until the struggle was over."

Solana rested her palms against the earth, feeling its steady pulse. "But healing isn't about erasing what was," she said. "It's about allowing what is to settle."

Seraphiel's wings glowed softly, casting gentle halos across the clearing. "The shadows didn't exist to defeat us," he said. "They existed to teach us how to carry the light without fear."

Silence followed — not heavy, not uncertain. A silence filled with recognition.

They had crossed fear. They had crossed doubt. They had learned that courage was presence, not force. That clarity was choice, not control. That healing was not fixing — but tending.

Aurelian looked at the others. Not assessing. Not protecting. Just looking — the way you look at people you have traveled with through the worst of yourself and found still standing on the other side. His eyes rested on Solana, who met his gaze without flinching. On Zophira, whose sharp features had softened into something closer to peace. On Seraphiel, who sat with his wings folded and his face open and unperforming. For the first time in memory, Aurelian existed in a space without a role. No one needed his protection. No threat required his vigilance. And the absence of duty did not feel like emptiness. It felt like arrival.

And now, the land agreed The River of Process brightened, its glow rippling outward — not in urgency, but in affirmation. Grass stirred where none had grown before. Wildflowers bloomed along the banks, their colors vivid and unhurried.

***

In the village

The change was felt before it was seen.

Villagers emerged from their homes, drawn by a warmth they could not name. The river glowed brighter, its steady rhythm calming hearts long accustomed to unrest.

Selene knelt at the water's edge, tears slipping free. "It feels… settled," she whispered.

She reached into the water and lifted a smooth stone — one of the ones Solana had carried in her pocket at the start of the journey, a name-stone, worn by months of river current. Selene did not know whose name it carried. She pressed it against her chest and held it, the way you hold a letter you have waited years to receive.

Maelis emerged from her loom-house, a length of freshly woven cloth draped over her arm. The threads had glided that morning for the first time in weeks — smooth, willing, whole. She did not know why. She simply folded the cloth and set it on the step for whoever needed it next.

Doran stood at the edge of his field. The soil was still thin, still scarred from the weeks of withering. But when he knelt and pressed his hand into the earth, it gave. It was warm. He closed his eyes and let himself believe, for one careful breath, that the land would yield again.

Elder Myrial stood beside her, hands folded, eyes shining. "Because the land is no longer asking to be saved," she said. "It's asking to be lived in."

Tovrik joined them at the riverbank. His hands were rough and his face was tired, but there was something in the set of his shoulders that had not been there for weeks — not hope, exactly. Readiness. The kind of stillness that comes before the first motion of rebuilding.

"The children are asking about the quartet," he said. "Wanting to know if they're coming home."

Myrial's eyes crinkled. "They are home," she said. "They just haven't walked through the gate yet."

The villagers moved — not in awe, not in fear, but with quiet purpose. They cleared debris from the riverbanks. They replanted fields. Elders worked alongside children, There were no commands given, no urgency imposed — only shared care.

The blacksmith's apprentice carried water to the miller's garden. The miller checked the weaver's roof where a beam had warped. Maelis brought the fresh cloth to Selene, who cut it into strips for bandaging — not because anyone was wounded, but because preparing for care was its own kind of hope. No one orchestrated it. No one directed. The village moved the way a body moves when it remembers how to breathe: one small motion leading to the next, each one sufficient, each one connected.

***

Back in the clearing

Solana pressed her hands into the soil.

Light flowed — not in waves this time, but in roots.

Green spread outward, steady and enduring. Aurelian rose, his presence anchoring the space — not as a shield, but as a cornerstone. Zophira stepped beside him, her clarity no longer searching for what might go wrong, but recognizing what was now right. Seraphiel unfurled his wings, their glow gentle, complete.

Solana pressed her hands into the soil one last time. She did not push warmth into the ground. She let the ground offer it to her — a slow, mineral heat that rose through her palms and settled in her chest like a held breath finally released. "I spent my whole life giving," she said quietly. "I didn't know receiving could feel this terrifying." She looked at her hands — marred, capable, open, and necessary."

Zophira stood at the river's edge, watching the current with the same sharp eyes that had always searched for threats and patterns. But now she saw something else: the river did not need to be mapped. It did not need to be understood. It needed to be trusted. She let her gaze soften. The water moved, and she did not try to read it. She simply watched. And for a woman who had built her identity on knowing, not-knowing felt like the bravest thing she had ever done.

Seraphiel's wings dimmed — not from exhaustion, but by choice. He folded them against his back and stood in the clearing without radiance, without performance. Just a man. The others did not look away. They did not ask him to shine. He felt seen in a way that light had never accomplished.

They stood together — not as warriors, not as saviors — but as keepers of balance.

The River of Process curved toward the village, its glow connecting land to land, shadow to light, past to present.

Zophira broke the quiet. "This part of the journey is complete." Solana smiled softly. "The land knows who it is again."

Seraphiel's wings shimmered. "And so do we."

Aurelian looked toward the horizon. Beyond the village, beyond the softened edge of the Dark Land, the world stretched wide — not demanding, not urgent. "Then we stay," he said. "For now."

He looked at each of them — Solana, whose empty hands had become her greatest offering. Zophira, whose sharpest sight had become the willingness to not-see. Seraphiel, whose truest light turned out to be the one he didn't perform. And he understood, finally, that his own strength had never been the shield. It was this: the ability to stand still in a world that no longer required his protection and found that he was enough without the weight.

The silence between them held no tension. It was not waiting to be filled. It was complete — the kind of silence that exists between people who have nothing left to prove to each other.

They did not rush forward. They did not turn back. They remained — present, whole, at peace.

And the Land of Soul breathed with them — in concord, in balance, in light.

Epilogue: THE RIVER THAT REMAINS

Seasons passed, and the Land of Soul learned how to breathe again. Not in bursts of urgency or fear, but in a steady rhythm — one that carried memory without being bound by it. The River of Process flowed as it always had, luminous and alive, winding through fields now softened by growth and care. Its waters reflected the sky, the land, and the people who had learned to listen to it once more.

The village changed — not all at once, not perfectly, but honestly. Children played along the riverbanks, their laughter light and unguarded. Elders worked beside them, hands in the soil, no longer standing apart as keepers of order but as participants in the living whole. Disagreements still arose, grief still visited, doubt still whispered — but none of it ruled the land anymore. The people had learned something essential: light did not mean the absence of shadow; healing did not mean the erasure of pain; balance did not mean stillness. It meant relationship.

At the heart of the village, a tree took root where the river curved wide. Its branches stretched outward, leaves shimmering faintly with gold and green. It was not planted in celebration, nor in remembrance — but in recognition. A living marker of a turning point that the land would not forget.

The quartet often returned to the river — not as guardians standing watch, but as witnesses to what had grown. Aurelian stood quietly at the water's edge, strength no longer measured by what he carried alone but by what he allowed to stand beside him. Zophira walked the paths with clear eyes and an open heart, wisdom no longer sharp with certainty but softened by humility. Solana knelt often in the fields, her healing no longer driven by urgency but by care that included herself. Seraphiel's light moved gently through the land, no longer blazing to be seen, but glowing because it was true.

They spoke less of what they had faced. Not because it was forgotten — but because it had been integrated. The Dark Land remained on the horizon, its presence no longer feared. Its shadows rested, no longer pressing forward, no longer denied. The River of Process flowed through it as well, unbroken, reminding all who looked upon it that growth required depth as much as light.

One evening, as the sun dipped low and the river caught fire with amber and gold, the quartet stood together once more. "This part is complete," Zophira said — not as a declaration, but as an acknowledgment. Solana smiled softly. "The land knows itself again." "And so do we," Seraphiel added, his wings catching the fading light. Aurelian looked beyond the river's bend, where the water disappeared into distance — not calling, not demanding. "Life will move again," he said. "It always does."

The river answered — not with words, but with motion. Steady. Enduring. Alive. And though no one stepped forward that night, the path remained — open, patient, waiting. Not because another journey was required. Because becoming never truly ends.

Years later, the tree at the river's curve bore small carved tokens — offerings left by villagers who had learned to mark both sorrow and joy. The children who once fled the starlings grew into storytellers who taught the next generation how to name shadows and tend light. The quartet taught apprentices, not to wield power, but to listen: to the river, to the land, and to the small, honest voices inside themselves. When storms came, the village met them with practiced care; when harvests failed, they sat together and named the loss, then planted again.

On certain mornings, the quartet would walk the riverbank in silence, each step a quiet vow: to keep tending, to keep remembering, to keep being present. The River of Process moved beside them, as it always had, carrying what was given and returning what was needed. The Land of Soul rested — in concord, in balance, in light. And the river flowed on.

Glossary Preface

Both the Land of Soul and the Dark Land are simultaneously literal places and metaphors for inner life; each shape and is shaped by the other.

Core Concepts

River of Process

Definition: The living current of growth, truth, and transformation that runs through both lands and through every person.

Essence: The River is necessary — nothing of lasting growth or integration happens without it; it carries memory, catalyzes change, and makes integration possible.

Narrative role: Mood meter, catalyst for turning points, and the structural engine of the story's moral work; crossings, rapids, and pools mark decisions, crises, and reflection.

Land of Soul

Definition: The village and the interior life it represents; — both a literal community and the inner landscape of the self.

Function: Shows how inner work ripples outward; the social field where integration is practiced, witnessed, and sustained.

Dark Land of the Soul

Definition: The interior terrain of fear, grief, and unresolved truth — dramatized as a place to traverse.

Function: Externalizes suppressed emotions and forces revelation; a necessary passage where awareness deepens and transformation begins.

Balance
Not stillness or perfection, but the ongoing relationship between light and shadow, truth and fear, self and world.

Presence
The act of staying with what is real — without rushing, fixing, or fleeing.

Integration
The moment when shadow and light coexist honestly and the land and self are no longer at war.

Quick Comparison Table

Aspect	Land of Soul	Dark Land of the Soul
Literal and figurative	Literal village; figurative inner life	Literal realm in story; figurative inner terrain
Primary tone	Community, tending, daily life	Testing, revelation, confrontation
Primary function	Shows social consequences of inner work	Forces confrontation with shadow for integration
Relationshi p to River	River nourishes and reflects communal health	River runs through it; shows depth of inner work

Main Characters and Interior Maps

Aurelian — Courage

Gift: Protective steadiness.
Wound: Identity tied to carrying others.

Work: Learn to share burden and ask for help; let courage be a shared ember.

Zophira — Clarity

Gift: Pattern sight and maps.
Wound: Overreliance on certainty.
Work: Hold questions; practice humility in knowing.

Solana — Healing

Gift: Tending, naming, holding grief.
Wound: Self erasure through endless giving.
Work: Learn to receive and tend herself as well as others.

Seraphiel — Light

Gift: Illumination and witness.
Wound: Shining to be needed.
Work: Shine from inner truth rather than survival.

Shadows and Figures — Negative and Positive Aspects

Shadow or Figure	Negative Aspect	Positive Aspect
Fearmonger	Amplifies anxiety and freezes action.	Signals real danger and protects when listened to wisely.
Wrathbearer	Consumes through suppressed rage and destructive outbursts.	Reveals boundaries and fuels necessary change when acknowledged.
Shadowkeeper	Hoards guilt and memory until it becomes a burden.	Preserves lessons and ensures the past is carried with honesty.
Apathetic Void	Numbs meaning and encourages surrender.	Creates space to rest and reassess priorities when engaged gently.
Perplexia	Overloads with doubt and paralyzing options.	Forces discernment and clarifies values

Shadow or Figure	Negative Aspect	Positive Aspect
Hollowshade	Drains emotional will and numbs the soul into passive surrender	Reveals the need for rest and creates space to reconnect with what truly matters
Shadowess	Reflects identity as fixed masks and defensive roles.	Mirrors hidden truths and invites authentic self naming.
Nyxalia	Confronts with raw emptiness that can feel annihilating.	Opens the threshold for deep revelation and true transformation.
Celeve	Can feel like harsh accountability if misapplied.	Holds compassionate accountability that integrates care with truth.

Cross References to Chapters

- River of Process: Chapters 3, 5, 10, 16, 20, 22, 23.
- Land of Soul (community scenes): Chapters 8, 12, 13, 20, 24.
- Dark Land trials: Chapters 3–7, 9–11, 14–19.
- Fearmonger encounters: Chapters 3, 12, 15, 21.
- Wrathbearer encounters: Chapters 7, 12, 15.
- Shadowkeeper encounters: Chapters 6, 12, 15.
- Apathetic Void / Hollowshade: Chapters 9, 10, 12.
- Perplexia and Shattered Paths: Chapters 10, 14, 21.
- Nyxalia and the Abyss: Chapters 18–19.
- Surrender and Integration: Chapters 16–17, 23–24.
- Village rituals and repair: Chapters 11, 20, 24, Epilogue.

A Note: Self-Discovery Companion Workbook

The Land of Soul Discovery Workbook was created as a gentle companion to this story. It offers space to reflect, explore, and integrate the truths that surfaced along the journey. There is no required pace and no expected outcome — only an invitation to meet yourself with honesty and care.

Acknowledgments

This book was born in quiet places.

In the pauses between breaths. In the moments when the shadows felt too heavy.

In the soft, persistent whisper that said,

Keep going.

To everyone who walked with me —

in spirit, in memory, in presence —

Thank you for holding space for my becoming.

To the ones who taught me about light,

and the experiences that taught me about Shadows.

Those lessons shaped every page.

To the people who reminded me that healing is not a destination but part of the journey toward wholeness —

To the readers who find themselves somewhere in these pages:

may you feel seen, accompanied, may you remember that your river of process is always moving,

even when the flow feels still.

To the land — both the one beneath my feet and the one within my soul —

Thank you for teaching me how to listen.

And finally, to the part of me that kept writing even when the path felt unclear:

I honor you.

I'm proud of you.

This book is a return, a remembering, a beginning.

Thank you for being part of it.

www.ingramcontent.com/pod-product-compliance
Lightning Source LLC
LaVergne TN
LVHW090524110826
845146LV00003B/978

9798995538608